The Dresden Gate

THE
DRESDEN
GATE

Michael Schmidt

Hutchinson

London   Melbourne   Auckland   Johannesburg

First published in Great Britain by Century Hutchinson & Co Ltd
Brookmount House, 62–65 Chandos Place, London WC2N 4NW

Century Hutchinson Group (Australia) Pty Ltd
16–22 Church Street, Hawthorn, Melbourne, Victoria 3122

Century Hutchinson Group (NZ) Ltd
PO Box 40–068, 32–34 View Road, Glenfield, Auckland 10

Century Hutchinson Group (SA) Pty Ltd
PO Box 337, Bergvlei, 2010, South Africa

Filmset in 11/12 pt Linotron Baskerville by
Rowland Phototypesetting Ltd
Bury St Edmunds, Suffolk
Printed and bound in Great Britain by
Anchor Brendon Ltd, Tiptree

ISBN 0 09 165510 2

For Claire Harman

Questi non hanno speranza di morte,
e la lor cieca vita è tanto bassa,
che invidiosi son d' ogni altra sorte.
Fama di loro il mondo esser non lassa,
misericordia e giustizia gli sdegna:
non ragionlam di lor, ma guarda e passa.

1

He was eight when his uncle took him to the very top of El Abanico. His father was too busy to come with them.

The carriage left the courtyard before dawn and plunged into the whispering darkness of the cane fields. Sunrise met them as they emerged on the lower slopes. While the shadows were still long they reached the broken road to the mine.

It elbowed upwards between pirul trees and cactuses – here a trench gouged deep in the mountain flank and, higher, a sheer causeway between outcrops. Little crosses by the wayside marked the graves of those who died in the building. Disuse, then the big earthquake of '91, had done for it.

They climbed on foot. When they broke through underbrush they left a wake of swirling yellow moths. It was very steep at the top and Tio Alex, though frail and hunched, half-carried and half-dragged the boy. At last they emerged panting on the ridge.

It was cool, despite the sun: midday, shadows were absorbed into their forms. They looked over the bleached plain. For Tio Alex, it was a map on which was printed the geography of failure: parched, picturesque, his brother's estate spilled over partly arid, partly silver hectares. All they had brought, all they had been, the land had drunk.

For the boy, it was a sea, and the hacienda rode on it like a ship. The long body of the house with high-arched windows, and the chapel with its tilting, uncompleted belfry, and the bulky stables and outbuildings of rusty stone rode at anchor. Beyond was the terra firma of the plain. When the rains came, stunted maize grew there, or a greenish skin would spread on

I

untilled ground and burst into yellow flower, then subside. Beyond the criss-crossed stone walls of dead fields, shale and sand stretched to the indistinguishable town of Santa Marta, a patch of smoke. Then further hills, blue-grey, another kind of world, a world of cloud.

The railway meandered across the plain. It might have run straight, but it had been built by 'interests' with pressing reasons to avoid straight lines. Once a week, trains made their passage to and fro from the Pacific up through the mountains, and four hundred miles (as the crow flies) to the capital. They passed within a mile of the hacienda. Don Raoul, the boy's father, had built a halt and a few stone sheds. It was the only thing he had added in his years there.

Tio Alex and the boy identified everything familiar – but the house, the chimneys, the seven scattered hamlets where the peons and their families lived islanded among the cane fields, the haze of Santa Marta (the railway line drew the eye to it) looked odd from such a height. So bald, so insignificant: those places of shade and rustling cane, the towering house, the old canals and riverbed, the reeking settlements.

They turned the other way, as if to seek relief in the unfamiliar. A strange chaos of fallen stones, steep to a valley without stain of green, a lower mountain opposite, a further valley . . .

They looked back at the plain. Flecks of men moved on paths and roads, a horseman raised puffs of dust. They were silent, quenched by the emptiness of the place.

The boy did not forget it, how shimmering and substanceless it was. He felt like one of the birds that spin above the plain and, dizzy at the summit, see El Abanico not as horizon but a point of vantage with other valleys beyond it.

He did not forget the mine, either. They walked along the ridge that sloped to the crest. The road once led to the big shafts there. At the top a kind of crown had been built, a crenelated enclosure wall at which the boy had often gazed from his window, believing it a castle.

They went in at the broken gateway to a compound, scaled a wall and, balancing with difficulty, raised themselves at last higher than everything else.

'If Father could see us!'

'He's gone to Santa Marta with the engineer.' It was about a

2

new canal. Tio pointed to the middle distance. If Don Raoul could get his canal built, all that desert would be sugar cane. If Don Raoul could get the finance for it. If he could persuade someone to look closely at his costings – but not too closely at the land.

'If he was to look up from the road to Santa Marta,' the boy insisted, 'he might see us as dots on top of this crown!' He took off his white straw hat and waved it at empty space. Then he glanced down and saw the drop before him, bearded cliff-plants straggling into a gulf of shadow. He edged back.

Tio sat down on the wall. He took out a slim cheroot and lighted it. The boy liked those pale sticks of acrid scent, not like the bitter smoke from his father's thick cigars, but subtler – mist rather than cloud.

Tio's voice was sad. 'What do you suppose this place was?' Before the boy could answer, he explained. Once upon a time it was like an anthill. More than a thousand men worked the mine. They lived somewhere nearby – he gestured to a slope of scrub and pepper trees. There was no trace of their habitations – flimsy places, entirely lost. Yet from that slope each day men climbed into the mouth of the shaft and were lowered with their tools into the mountain. There were mules that lived in there and went blind with years of dark. The gold mine drove more than a mile into the earth, and the enormous slide of shale and loose stone behind them, where plants did not take root, was brought up with the ore. Big wagons bore the good rock down the mountain by the route they had climbed. El Abanico was modest beside the mines of Guanajuato, yet it had been enough for one family's fortunes. It had occasioned a huge meander in the railway line. It had turned hunters, peasants, shamans, even fishermen from the coast, into ants, with its promise of work in the hard years before Independence and the harder years that followed.

But the mine died. Tio Alex was not clear why it had died, but quite suddenly, forty years back, it had stopped bleeding wealth for the Obermullers. The broken chapel through which they were walking was stripped of its icons and let rent-free to weather.

One day it stopped. Men scattered down the hill and built their hamlets. They ceased to be ants and became worms

3

instead, spreading cane fields like lichen on the surface of the plain. The Obermullers remained their masters. Perhaps the price of gold fell, or a rich seam was worked out. Or someone determined that there was easier money in sugar. Whatever the reason, Tio disagreed. When he had first joined his brother at La Encantada, he had urged him, begged him to open the mountain again, even if hc did so only experimentally, with a score or two of men. The mountain was a part of the estates, after all. Ledger books going back more than a hundred years proved what it yielded. But Don Raoul had never set foot on this summit. No one had come but Tio Alex.

'I always thought this stone crown was a castle,' the boy said, trying to conceal his disappointment.

'Not *here*, child. There are no castles here.'

They walked around the compound. It had lost its magic but the boy listened respectfully to his uncle who seemed to feel that here, in these ruins, the future lay. The excursion was a chapter in the boy's education, a meek subversion of his father's will.

A clock-bird burst out of the mesquite and hopped on to a wall, its tail flickering. It cried and dropped into the gorge. Iguanas lay stunned on the yellow stone.

'From below, it *looks* like a great castle.' The boy stared down on the sea, the stranded ship. It was his house. The weekly train was spilling white cloudlets across the fields, stealing forward without sound, so slowly you could not be sure it was moving at all.

'You can see everything from here.'

The boy shook his head but looked so that his uncle would not see how he felt cheated. The world his father kept was small and poor.

His uncle hobbled along the stones like a crippled bird, now leaping up, now back.

'I told your father his fortune was here, under our feet, our hands. What they got from here bought the Obermullers the *campo* as far as Santa Marta. It built the canals, it planted the cane and maize. In a few years we could be rich, as rich as they were, and live as we did when we first came. Your father doesn't listen to Tio Alex. He keeps thinking about water, and sugar, and maize. He keeps his nose in ledger books and believes the weather will befriend him one day. When the place is yours, remember what I say. Your fortune isn't on the flat. It's behind the house, behind the fields, in the rock above you.'

They looked at the way they had come and at the solid ruins that surrounded them. Breeze spun the dust in little funnels that danced from wall to wall.

Suddenly it didn't look quite so straightforward. 'The cost will be large,' Tio Alex conceded. But his eyes were on the profit. There could be a future. He stamped a foot on the ground, scooped up pebbles in his smooth hands and sifted them. The breeze winnowed out the dust.

'We must go, if we're to get home before nightfall.'

They hurried along the ridge to the plunging road. A wind was rising.

'I thought it was a castle,' the boy repeated, half aloud. They clambered down in silence to where the carriage waited for them. The horses were asleep in the sparse pirul shade. How hot the lower slope still was! Higher up, nearer to the sun, it had been cool.

They got home with the dark. Don Raoul was not yet back from Santa Marta.

2

There was no light in Don Raoul's tower room – the boy
thought of it as the lantern of the ship – from which the *patron*
surveyed his world. The great hull lay quite still, quite dark
except for Tia Thérèse's barred window. At night there was
always a glow from there. Either she feared the dark or she
never slept. All day, barred light fell across her patterned
carpet, and all night, her room spilled back a grillwork shadow.
It was as though she were waiting.

Even the kitchens were dark. The servants lay on their straw
mattresses and snored.

Just a hint of light came from the chapel. No one had been
instructed to keep the hanging altar lamp lighted, but it burned
and no questions were asked. Silent Marie, the barefoot servant
who never said a word, who had been at La Encantada since the
time of the Obermullers and survived as their ghost, pale and
biddable, was suspected: it must have been she who got oil from
Santa Marta, out of her own poor wages or money teased off
from the domestic budget. She was devout, wearing her rosary
on her wrist and shaping the *Ave* with her lips. Tio Alex
imagined her at midnight, up a ladder with her little phial – one
of the wise virgins, but to what end? The host had not been
consecrated in that musty spiritual pantry since before Paula
decamped, taking the heart of the place with her.

The carriage spun in at the tall Dresden gate and drew up in
the courtyard, clattering, its horses snorting, splashing the light
of its fixed lamps on the cobblestones. The door of the house did
not fly open. No footman stood by with a lantern to greet them,
no stable boys ran to grab the bridles. Tio Alex pried the

carriage door open and lowered his half-asleep nephew to the ground. He tumbled down himself and called '*Buenas noches*' to the driver. A whip flicked and they were left in silence. Out of his pocket Tio Alex drew a key as long as a dagger, lit a match to find the keyhole, engaged the mechanism, and the big door opened.

They were home.

Such light-headedness as Tio Alex had brought back from the mountaintop vanished in the stale hallway. He led the boy by the hand to his room. Without lighting a candle, the child undressed and lay on his bed. Nothing detained him: he went to sleep.

Tio Alex lighted a cheroot and followed its glow down the corridors to his own rooms. His bed had not been made. He threw open the window, propped his elbows on the sill, and stared towards the mountains. He watched the red spot of his cigar, the haze it made, and the dim line between peaks and sky. The stars were piled up high. There was no moon. At last, naked, he took his place where he had broken off his dreams before dawn, before the excursion, in the tumbled bed. He coughed hard: the dust had made mud in his lungs. Then, like his nephew, he too fell asleep.

3

When Tio Alex first arrived at La Encantada, it had been a different world. His brother had inherited the Obermuller staff of footmen, doorman, servants, gardeners, maids. Arrivals and departures were still public events. Doors slammed, footsteps hurried down the long passages. As soon as you left your room in the morning, the bed was aired; your boots were always polished and set out by your door at daybreak; the ewer was always filled with spring water, even during the dry months. Mealtimes were long engagements for the household – interminable, they seemed to Don Raoul, who was a man impatient, busy, keen to make his fortune. His impatience, and the reluctance of his fortune to come good, led to a thinning out of the servants. Even before Paula departed, the scale on which they lived became more humble.

In the early months, Tio Alex rode out daily with Don Raoul, on a good mount, feeling important as the *patron*'s younger brother. They argued and laughed together. Alex had entertained the ladies well – so well that Tia Thérèse began to get ideas. He explored, looked for adventures, as though his weak lungs had been a spur. He felt he had stepped back into the nineteenth century. Life had never been so full for him – the *café* world of Paris grew remote. Here he felt he might find a vocation.

He began sketching once more, indifferently but profusely, in little leather-backed notepads, and both Paula and Thérèse admired his work. In the evenings he wrote out his discoveries about the history of the place and its geology – especially the geology that related to the mountain, and the history that related to its yield. How he tired them with his researches! He spent hours among the old ledgers in his brother's tower room, copying out the records of the mine.

His interest in the place went beyond statistics. The peons began to emerge from their landscape and to put on faces. He learned to call not only the domestic servants but the Indians from the nearest village by their names. He greeted them and tried to penetrate their dialect. He wrote poems. The love poems he had written in Paris had always been short and insipid as the affairs that gave rise to them – Parnassian, he called them. His long verse meditations on history, flora, fauna, exile, were at least different. He gave them up before he quite found his natural idiom, but not before he had bored the ladies with his recitations.

They used to sing quite passably to his accompaniment, especially Thérèse when she was in the mood.

But Paula left. Even before her departure, he began to be bored by La Encantada. He responded to his new life as a convert might do to a new faith. There was grace in the seeming prosperity of his brother's world, compared with the modest student existence he had endured in Paris. There was grace in the love he had for his relations. But it wore thin. The prosperity proved thin, the love wore thin. The weather had a cruel monotony and his researches became repetitive. He travelled to the capital not only to consult doctors about his chest. He went there for the busy streets, for the cafés and bookstores, for the echoes he heard of a life he had been glad to abandon.

He still rode out, now with his nephew riding behind him, not with his brother who had become so engrossed in his failure that he could spare only an occasional civility, sensing that Tio Alex had begun to pity him.

Tio Alex enjoyed showing the boy the tracks and roads through the cane fields, and how they changed. He taught him what he knew about the land, about the language. He showed him how to use the various firearms that hung on the walls of La Encantada like obsolete trophies. They brought home small game that the servants removed to the pantry with disgust.

Occasionally they bathed in old canals where the water was tepid and greened with moss. Or they visited the large village east of the hacienda with its squat church and thatched shacks. While the boy amused himself in the shade, Tio, hat in hand,

9

talked for half an hour with the priest, a shy, white figure who kept out of the way of his flock, preferring to sit in the patio of his house as if safe under a stone, by the crooked mango tree that alone yielded sweetness here, turning pages of a book. It never looked to be a book of prayer. The stench of the village was oppressive: if they stayed too long, Tio Alex retched and coughed all the way back, cursing the typhus he was sure lived in such bad air.

Or uncle and nephew waited at the railway halt. The black engine sighed and stopped. Parcels for La Encantada were thrown down: a parcel of haberdashery and a letter for Tia Thérèse, magazines for Tio Alex, bulletins and bills for Don Raoul. Tio Alex was the self-appointed postman, expectant at each arrival, always disappointed, though he could not have said what miracle, what deliverance he waited for.

The train guard exchanged news with him. 'When are you coming away with us, Don Alejandro?' the driver shouted. They sat at a little table in one of the shacks and passed half an hour with coffee, or brandy that Tio Alex poured out of his silver flask. He used to tell them when he travelled to the capital that he would soon go home for good, to France. But 'soon' was flexible. Each month they teased him more gently. He was becoming threadbare, his beard and moustache were no longer carefully trimmed, his cheeks were hectic, his eyes shone unnaturally like those of a baby. He was the kind of man who began to die when he ceased to be vain and found the mirror unfriendly. When he first arrived at La Encantada with his sister-in-law and her cousin, full of swagger, pale as a ghost, what a figure he had cut! – not handsome, but deliberate and poised to the tips of his steep eyebrows. 'At least the *campo* has put colour in his face.'

He did not look older, precisely. Bachelors don't age – they change, they thicken, alter pace. Time treats them differently from other men, whether peons or *hacendados*. Isolation and disease devour them, but not time. Paris grew bright again in his mind: he felt he could go back tomorrow and find it unchanged, the spaces he had left there would not have silted up, the friends and lovers would be waiting, suspended, as they were in memory.

He watched his brother battle with the estate, grizzled,

haunted and alone. That was not his fate: no wife would ever desert him, no child sap his marrow. The struggles he assisted in here, the lives to which he ministered, were not his. Apart from the boy, who had devolved upon him. Even so, he was free to go if he wished. But he did not go.

The guard and the engine driver knew Don Alex would stay put. The family's exile was for good. You could tell that from a distance. The house looked as if great lichens grew on the stone; there was a feeling of rust about the railway halt itself. After the *zafra*, when the cane was loaded on the trucks, the yield dwindled year by year. The villages stank of excrement, the hacienda of failure.

Ever since Tio Alex was a child, his brother had commanded him. When Raoul requested his modest capital to pursue projects in the New World, the young man did not hesitate. When Raoul wrote that things went badly, he took the hint and came straight from his mild bohemian life, bringing his sister-in-law whom he loved absolutely and her companion, Thérèse, who fell in love with him. He gave up his future – such as it was – to the higher authority of his brother's will. A true bohemian would have sent his best regards. In Tio Alex there was a stray Roman gene.

He would go back only with the others, when their fortune was banked, when the estate was sold. But who would buy La Encantada? It had grown too poor. Besides, there were rumours. The train driver said that the army was nervous at the port and in the capital. The latest photographs of the Dictator showed Methuselah surrounded by advisers even older, all with Prussian beards combed over their chests.

'They are all deaf,' the guard said.

Tio Alex nursed his bad breathing and watched himself weaken by degrees. The doctor in Paris said a dry climate would make an immortal of him. Certainly he was dying more slowly than before. But after riding out, the flavour of dust settled in his throat and he coughed for hours. Then he took to his bed and tried to sleep.

He disliked children, but the boy had become his distraction. This was his brother's son, with the mother's pretty face.

Left alone with him, Tio Alex learned to play. He invested his leisure in the boy until days, dust and heat became tolerable.

He could wake up without disappointment and go to sleep with anticipation. 'He is almost my son.' Impatient, goaded by his failure, Raoul was hardly a father. Alex still believed in him with the forgiving fealty of a younger brother, but he saw the boy as an orphan, abandoned by his mother after two ugly years at La Encantada. Who was there to care for him? Not Thérèse, always buttoned into high-necked black like a widow. Raoul kept her on out of habit, and because he could not easily afford to ship her home. There was also the forlorn hope that she might bring Paula back from France – if indeed she had ever got there – and the suspicion that those letters that reached her came from Paris, that Thérèse still linked her to them.

She had tried to show an interest in the child. But she had wished that her cousin might produce a daughter. She tried to consider the little boy as a niece. Until he was seven, he spent hours in her room, especially when Tio was unwell or away in the capital. She took him into her confidence, dressed him in little costumes she devised, tying his hair with a ribbon.

'Tio is ill, is he?' she would say with satisfaction, unable to conceal her curiosity. 'I shall have you all to myself, then.' She closed the door. They shared a secret.

He sat on a stool at her feet, half-lost among the folds of her dress, struggling to embroider curious flowers she suggested. She lost patience with his stubborn hands and chided him. But when she dressed and combed him, she used another tone, touching his face with fingers that were almost warm.

Tio Alex was voluble. Even when they were trotting through the fields and half the words were lost on the wind, he talked. With Tia Thérèse whole hours passed in silence, and it seemed natural that this should be so. But suddenly she would say: 'What does Tio Alex teach you?' And not listening to his reply, she would ask: 'Does he ever speak of Paris?' Then: 'What does he think of the terrible heat we've been having?' Her face hung above his like a pitted moon. 'Does he talk to you about your mother?' She made the boy blouses, petticoats and frills, using her best lace. He loved Tia Thérèse. He knew he did not have to answer her questions.

'Bad, bad, bad!' she cried, snatching his needlework from him. 'I shall have to unpick it!' And his thorny red flower, which ought to have been a chastened little rose, was snipped out, the cloth in its frame handed back to him all blank again. He was accustomed to her temper. Perhaps he did have ten thumbs. She made him work on flowers unlike any he had ever seen in nature, composed of little mounded squares. The needle hurt his fingers.

'Does Tio Alex still wear those hideous green cravats?' She could have watched Tio Alex simply by looking from her window or, when he passed along the corridor with his walking stick, by peeping through the crack in the door. But she preferred to imagine him, at a safe remove.

The boy squinted at his needlework until his head ached.

'How is this, Tia?'

'Not right. Better, but not right, my dear. What *are* you doing with those long stitches?'

He started again, again failed. She fixed a new pattern in the frame.

'It's no use crying. *This* is how it is done.'

In an instant, it seemed, a regular pattern emerged. She made it precisely as a machine would have done. There were dozens of embroidered cushions on the bed, on the low window-seat. Over the years she had filled her room with flowers, all roses, pink and red, but scented with lavender.

'How is Tio Alex's chest?'

She opened her monthly parcels of haberdashery with trembling hands. Tio Alex brought them from the halt and left them at her door, along with any letters. He tapped gently and went away, and when she was sure the corridor was empty, she darted out and got them. She paid her own bills, out of what Tio called her 'spinster's dowry' – enough for little luxuries but too little to get her even as far as the coast by train.

Don Raoul resented her letters. He wanted to intercept them but Alex would not let him. He was certain they came from Paula, and Tia Thérèse replied to each missive at length – a secret agent, hunched half the night writing in a pool of lamplight, the edge of the spindly table that supported the water jug and basin pressing against her heart.

Sometimes she allowed the boy to explore the room. He was not tall enough to see out the window, but he could handle the frayed velvet of the curtains. He drank in the close fragrance that surrounded her, air that never changed because she never

13

let the window be opened, afraid of dispersing the various sweetnesses. There was the texture of the cloths in her large bureau, all folded away, the little rainbows of silk and tulle. Her black gowns, re-hemmed a dozen times, hung limply in the mirror-faced wardrobe. He touched them curiously, hesitant.

He never climbed into her lap and laid his cheek against her bosom. An edge of reserve kept them apart. Then sometimes she would sing in a pretty, sad voice ballads she'd heard as a girl, which spilled from memory.

> *Three little drummer boys*
> *Were coming home from war.*
> *One boy marched behind*
> *And two boys marched before.*
> *The two in front played on*
> *As though the war was won;*
> *The third boy, pale and drawn*
> *Played with the sticks no more.*
> *He marched on lame and wan*
> *And played with the sticks no more.*

If he asked her to sing, she refused. She always started unexpectedly, out of a long, confiding silence. And just as suddenly, she stopped.

Beside the canopied bed that occupied a quarter of her room hung a rank of cameo photographs arranged in an oval to which no face could be added. It was her finished family. She gave them names – cousins, real aunts, an uncle, his grandparents and great-grandparents, his mother.

He had no memory of her, so he gazed long at the face, a girl's, photographed when she was in her early teens, her skin a pure shadow and her eyes candid under slightly pointed brows. How firm her lips were! His aunt's, by contrast, were a crimson slit; his mother pouted in a reluctant smile.

Tia told him the names of the portraits, but nothing of their lives. 'I have forgotten. It is years and years ago.' It hurt her if he asked, so he wondered instead.

Above the bed, on the brocaded headboard, a plain cross hung, and a little hook held a rosary. She never told her beads when he was there, and the missal by her bed, her only book, was thick with dust.

4

Neither the reticence of Tio Alex nor the neglect of Don Raoul had altered Tia Thérèse. It was Paula's departure. Thérèse had been abandoned, widowed. It was her loss, the child should have fallen to her care, a memento. She wrote to France, perhaps to Paula herself, to say how the child was happy. She showed him how to walk prettily in the pretty clothes she made him, cutting up the remains of the wardrobe that had come with her to La Encantada when she consented to be her cousin's companion. Quite properly, her wardrobe had been only a shadow of Paula's, for she was herself a shadow. But it had its elegance and the boy liked the cool, sleek fabrics against his skin and admired in her glass the other child she made him, colouring his lips and cheeks with rouge. He looked as his mother had done as a girl. It did Tia Thérèse good to see him.

Who told Don Raoul? Not the boy: he spoke with his father only formally, hands clasped behind his back and staring at the floor, or stammeringly at dinner, with his uncle present. Thérèse herself would not have mentioned it: she knew her conduct would seem odd, however harmless in fact. She spoke to Don Raoul only at Easter to say 'God be with you,' and at Christmas.

Someone told Don Raoul.

One day, when Tio Alex, felled by a coughing fit, lay sweating in his dark room, the boy walked up and down before his aunt, wearing a pretty gown. She sat absolutely still, admiring how she had bound his hair, and the slope of neck and shoulder.

The door opened quietly. The smell of cigar smoke alerted her. Don Raoul stared at the girl in the flowered gown as if at something intensely familiar. He almost smiled with recognition.

'She is so like,' said Tia Thérèse, recovering herself.

He recognized his son. Stepping forward, he slapped his face, tore the fabric off the shoulders, jerked the ribbons from the hair. The boy stood half-naked before the two adults.

'He is mine, Thérèse. Remember that.' Then, to the boy, 'Go to your room and scrub your face.'

The boy ran down the corridor. He felt that he was burning: his face, his shoulders flared. He did not know why he was being punished. And why was Tia Thérèse being punished? The sound of her crying and of his father's voice followed him to his room. He slammed the door behind him.

After that, she hardly spoke to him again. If he knocked their agreed three times on her door, she did not answer. Occasionally he saw her moving through the house, but she did not even nod to him. He had ceased to exist. The only person she acknowledged was the servant Marie, who came and went with eyes averted, barefoot, diligent, respectful, almost invisible. Straightening a picture – those towering portraits of the Obermullers, those landscapes that translated the *campo* into a Prussian idiom – or gazing at the surfaces of dust on tables and sills, Tia Thérèse moved rigidly, with only the mirrors to appreciate her. It was as though she had stepped down from one of the frames, escaped the toils of art to move briefly into the air and disturb the falling dust. 'She has all the time in the world to be devout,' Tio Alex said. 'Women in her position cannot afford to be so secular.' The boy no longer loved her. Tio watched the way in which he cooled towards her.

At last she stayed in her room.

The boy still wished to see her photographs. The image of his mother troubled him.

'You knew my mother, Tio Alex.'

'Yes,' his uncle replied, but nothing more.

Tio Alex fell casually into the role of tutor. It was not a formal thing, simply that he was bored, and there was no one else to take the child in hand. And the child attached himself. No one suggested it, no one forbade it. Don Raoul trusted his brother and was amused to watch his son climb on to his brother's lap when he was reading. Tio Alex reflected that his nephew would be better company if he could read. He found a mild vocation, as teacher.

'And you, Margarita,' he asked at first, 'will you join us and become a scholar? There are enough books, I can get another slate. You can both share me.'

But Margarita, the boy's nurse, a fair girl turning twenty, declined. 'I am too old, Don Alejandro.'

'You are not so very old, my dear. But please yourself.'

He was rather glad she did not join them. When Paula had abandoned them, the baby fell to Margarita's charge though she was only in her early teens. Tio Alex had always liked her: she was cheerful and resourceful. She also grew prettier year by year. Though she was an Indian, she had the yellow hair that sometimes occurred in natives of the area – a residue of France. When Maximilian's army retreated, the fleeing *tricolor* passed this way. The soldiers left no names, but their features kept recurring.

Margarita seemed almost a relation. The more time he spent in company with her and the boy, the more she troubled him. She represented a danger to which he was no longer equal. 'I haven't the energy for this,' he said, and vanished for a glum month in the capital. On his return, he kept to himself, watching the boy grow and the girl turn into a woman. He saw how his brother watched her, too. When he began educating the boy, Margarita returned to the servants' quarters.

Tio taught by ridicule and laughter. He expected rapid progress, and his expectations were fulfilled. The boy wrote legibly, a round hand like his mother's. He read passably, then well.

They began the day with Latin, then spent an hour on French, another on mathematics or science, another on history. They spent six or seven hours together over books, or walking and riding through the fields. They were never silent. Whenever there was occasion, Tio Alex spoke about farming and husbandry, about which he knew little and spoke largely, and also the duties of a son. He liked to tell the boy about his father – how skilled he had been as a young man, how successful, how commanding. Thus Tio Alex indulged in an oblique confession of his own inadequacies, the reasons for his being at La Encantada.

'You knew my mother, Tio Alex,' the boy repeated. The only effect of his refrain was to divert the natural flow of their conversation.

Tio Alex set great store by the *Georgics*. Virgil might not be precisely accurate about country matters, yet he had got his hands dirty and his poetry was wise – wise in its elegance and in its substance. 'The bees we have here are not like Virgil's bees. He knew the fruitful bees of Italy . . . He was full of old saws and superstitions. Also a burden of legend. It's hardly just that such lines should contain so many errors.' The poem took Tio Alex home to the Mediterranean.

They had come to the line '*pastor Aristaeus fugiens Peneia Tempe*'.

> *. . . He stood by the stream and spoke.*
> '*Mother, Cyrene, embodiment of clear water,*
> *Is this what it means to be the son of a god?*'

'Why are you crying? It is only a poem about bees.'

> '*Bring him down to us, bring him down, since it is allowed*
> *That he cross into our mystery.*'

'It is not allowed,' said Tio Alex severely, troubled all the same by the boy's misery. He hadn't cried for the shepherd in the *Eclogues*, the one who died; and he could wager that when Dido threw herself on the pyre, the boy would not be so moved. But the spoiled brat Aristaeus touched him. They closed the book and left the poem unfinished. Tio Alex talked about other things; the boy gazed through the foliage at the plain. It was great and vacant. You could not see the sun but the slow combustion of dust rising, without any wind, making the sky tan. The railway line glowed opal like a river flowing away.

5

They advanced across the sands of learning crabwise, by digression. However intent Tio Alex might be on Cicero or Chénier or describing an astrolabe, the boy would set obstacles in his path. A question, a comment, and Tio Alex began to reminisce, just as an old man might. And after he had been going for a time, he stopped himself abruptly and turned back to the book like an ascetic who has indulged an exquisite, brief vice.

So the boy learned about his grandparents who lived in the south by the sea and sometimes went with their children to Italy. Tio remembered each detail of their small estate with clairvoyant accuracy: the olive groves and their blue-grey shade, the little twisted apple trees, village snickets, grape arbours, the dog that stayed with the family for 'fifty years – well, perhaps a little less'. The servants, teachers, cousins – all had names. When he spoke of them, his eyes gazed inwards on a stage whose properties had retained the sunrise brilliance of childhood, sweetened a little beyond nature by nostalgia.

Their tutorials were conducted on the balcony that opened off the tall formal room that had been Paula's sitting room, and which when she left was renamed the nursery. Foliage of hanging plants shaded them in the open air against the afternoon, and there were pots of azaleas that Tio Alex tended 'like a peasant – they're my fruitless orchard'. He was proud, too, of the bougainvillaea and the thick-stemmed grape vine that climbed out of its tub and formed a kind of arbour, reconstituted from his earlier world. They sat side by side on a bench, a table and piles of books before them.

Talking in the dappled shade, they watched, unseen themselves, the peons preparing fields for maize, donkeys laden with
cut sugar cane at *zafra*, occasionally an unknown horseman
passing, and Don Pepe, the overseer, always galloping somewhere, then galloping back. The train, too, once a week ascending, once descending, on the meander of rails. If there was a
wind from the west, fumes from the railway reached them. Tio
went indoors, a handkerchief to his face, and they continued
their lessons in the tall nursery, sitting before an empty grate.

In the open air, there were other perils. Sometimes a scorpion
flipped out from beneath a plant-pot, and bees came to inter-
rupt their reading, buzzing at the clusters of grapes and
clinging to the fuchsias. A bee flew into Tio Alex's hair and he
sat like a statue for half an hour, talking all the time, until it
found its way out behind his ear and, free of the web, buzzed
indignantly around his face. The boy was not so brave. When a
bee approached him, he ran inside and hid behind a curtain.

Their privacy was sometimes interrupted. Above them was
Don Raoul's lantern room with its wide windows. Though the
arbour was dense enough to shield them from the *patron*'s gaze,
they could hear his voice instructing Don Pepe. The words were
indistinct, but there was the even hum of Don Raoul's voice,
punctuated by the occasional shrill '*Si!*' of the servant, a man
who wore enormous spurs and a black sombrero and rode the
tall black horse tethered in the courtyard below.

Don Pepe was Don Raoul's right hand, merciless with that
brutality that gives the appearance of efficiency. But his voice
was that of a woman. Asked for advice, he habitually looked
grave and said nothing. Once instructed, he rode out at the
Dresden gate as if pursued. The peons fell back against the
walls or retreated into the sloping cane as he spurred his horse
out of sight. For those above him, Don Pepe was a source of
amusement. His inferiors did not risk a smile.

The boy watched the horse in the courtyard picking at the
dry grass between the cobbles. The courtyard was wide and
bare, bounded by a whitewashed arcade. It had been built as
a fortified enclosure when the mine was prospering. The
Obermullers tried to give it style, but achieved the scale and
charm of a parade ground. Don Raoul had tried to make it
homely, planting along the far wall a score of orange trees

which had not prospered but sent their desperate branches in every direction, with only a few clutches of leaves.

Like the house, the courtyard accommodated each generation in a different way. It had the suggestive incompleteness of the hacienda itself, recording a succession of intentions, but always disowning the domestic scale, the human measure, without achieving the monumental or aristocratic. It was a half-way house between the bourgeoisie and real blood – a half-way house from which no road led forward.

Three wings opened off the main hall. A visitor, lost in the corridors that strung the apartments together, described La Encantada as a hive. Some of the remote rooms were storage places; some were abandoned with the stucco falling in slabs. Through other little bedrooms and boudoirs a servant moved each week, keeping the absence dusted. The curtains remained closed except in the lived-in central rooms, so that the fabrics would not fade. This gave the house from the outside the aspect of mourning.

Don Raoul had added latticed shutters. They had been painted white but now were tinder-dry and flaking, absorbing the yellow of the stone. When he arrived, he had wanted to make the sharp edges of his palace more gentle. 'We will translate this Prussian into French,' he had told Tio Alex. He had planted poplars but a single summer did for them. Around the courtyard, he had placed low-backed benches so that on summer evenings he and his bride could sit and watch the sky. The time never came for that.

The cobbles in the courtyard traced the pattern of a giant flower, the stone petals spreading from a fountain at the heart to the edges of the square. The fountain, the diminutive corolla of the flower, was goblet-shaped. Its grey stone bowl was almost six feet wide, rimmed with geometrical foliage. The fountain jet no longer played, though when Tio Alex first arrived it still shot out a thin gesture of water, and there were goldfish and the pancake leaves of lilies. In summer the lilies were baked yellow on top like native corncakes. During the day the fish lay stunned with heat, but in the evening they broke the surface with their mouths. Now the skin of soil along the bottom of the bowl was deep enough for little weeds to root in the rainy season.

Along the front of the courtyard ran a false arcade of high arches bricked in and whitewashed, a fortress wall. There was a side gate. The triumphal central arch pierced the wall and opened to the road, framing Santa Marta in the distance. In this archway, on huge hinges, hung the iron gate – a gift sent to the first Herr Obermuller by his father-in-law, a mayor of Dresden. Even the peons called it the Dresden gate.

Heinrich Obermuller built the original hacienda, a low rambling house, primitive but suited to his needs. The mine at El Abanico was sending down first a trickle, then a stream of treasure from the heights. The thick-walled rooms were cool and secure. He raised a high arcade around the courtyard to protect against marauding Indians and bandits.

When he sent for his wife, she crossed the sea in the same ship as his father-in-law's extraordinary gift. Wife and gate arrived together, drawn overland – it was before the British engineers built the railway line – one in a sturdy coach, the other on a huge wagon pulled by mules and guarded by an escort of militia who were well-rewarded for their pains. Herr Obermuller was becoming famous.

For him, the arrival of the woman and the gate marked a change. Frau Obermuller complained. She complained about the length of her journey. She complained about her back, her skin, her fingers, and most of all about the poverty of her accommodation. She came out in a rash that disfigured her face for a year. She was homesick. She threatened to leave.

Her husband spent the rest of his life between the mine and his wife, exploiting one, exploited by the other. Much of the mountain's yield was invested in bringing the fruits and medicines of Europe to the woman. The house grew taller by two storeys, almost worthy of her ambitions, and of the Dresden gate.

She died before the third wing was complete, complaining still. But she left an heir.

The gate became a symbol for the Obermullers, as valuable to their self-esteem as a title would have been. The gate opened backwards in time, to the old country. The last Obermuller, Otto, stepped through it as if through a magic window when he returned to his fatherland. He sold up to Don Raoul and put five generations of his family behind him. They lay abandoned in the chapel vault.

The Dresden gate drew the eye like an exotic flower in a drab garden. It *was* magnificent: no effort of the Obermullers or of Don Raoul could make La Encantada worthy of it. It reproached its surroundings. Alexander von Humboldt had paused before it respectfully, making a note of it in his chronicle of the remarkable things of New Spain.

Don Raoul kept the keys of the main gate on a chain that hung at his waist. Only when the carriage was in use was the gate opened. The side gate served for daily use, standing open night and day, and was high enough to admit a horseman.

From the balcony the boy could see, over the top of the Dresden gate, the long dusty road flowing into haze. On either side the fields were marked off in irregular squares by stone walls. In another season they would be green and red with maize; now they were dust.

The dust stuck to his fingers where he rested them on the balustrade; it drifted into the house each day. The servants dabbed at it but it returned. Tia Thérèse used to call the servants 'slackers'. But now she sat, as the boy had done, and watched how the dust gathered, coming in through the ill-fitting windows, settling first here and there, a flake or two, but in an hour – or less if there was a breeze – laying its skin over everything. The boy had watched it gather in the sunlight on tables and on panes. He had watched the servants with their vegetable patience catching it up in a cloth, carrying it away, freeing it from a window. Back it came. Wherever one laid a hand, the dust was there.

The voice of Don Raoul fell silent overhead. Don Pepe's spurs rang on the stairs. He burst from the door below the balcony, whipped his horse's tether from the rail and leapt into the saddle. Bowing his head, he galloped out through the pedestrian gate, turned left and vanished along the blind arcade, reappearing briefly where the side road led into the cane fields.

How different that view was from the northern prospect – the enormous grey-green lake of cane and, beyond, the gentle slopes, the jagged foothills of El Abanico, and behind them the huge fan of the mountain itself. Breeze in the cane gave motion

23

even to the shimmering stone permanence. The grey-green light below, the brown light above, and over the rim of the fan – so cruelly painted with sharp cliffs and spilled forests – the sky, whitish where the mountain touched it but, as the eye turned up (the way an eye is said to turn in death, but before it slides beneath the lid), there, overhead, the amazing pure blue of the dome.

'When shall we climb to the mine again, Tio Alex?'

'One day, one day.'

But in the years that had passed since their first expedition, Tio Alex had weakened. He seldom rode out even to the railway halt, and when they went walking, sometimes he had to lean on the boy's shoulder, or take his silver-headed walking stick, once a toy of vanity.

'The cool would do you good. Remember how it was cool when we got to the top? There was no dust in the air.'

They went in from the balcony. The room was full of shadows. They did not take up their reading again but sat talking about other things. Then Marie, silent as a shadow, came and laid out their meal on the large writing table, and they ate.

6

The boy had his mother's face. It pained Don Raoul to look at him. But a change would come. He kept an eye on him. When he walked with Tio Alex in the courtyard, the father stood at his window, remote and curious. Or he listened to the murmur of their voices when they pursued their studies on the balcony, invisible beneath the arbour leaves. He heard no words, only animated tones.

He asked Tio Alex for reports.

'Why is the boy always alone? He should play with other children.'

'There are only the peons. Would you have him play with their children?'

'They could be brought to the house – at least into the courtyard, I suppose.'

Chickens had found their way from the kitchen garden into the courtyard and were pecking at the cobbles. Sun shone blindingly on the open space. It was a parade ground, impersonal, intolerably hot.

'Not a very cheerful place for playing,' Tio Alex suggested.

'He cannot go to them. It would be unhealthy to send him to the village. They must come here.'

'Why do you say *they*? One or two friends could be found.'

'I do not speak of friends. I speak of play, of exercise. A number will be best. They can –' he considered what they could do, '– run about.' He was vague but emphatic. 'The boy reads too much. Remember the work he will have to do. He should be made strong.'

Don Raoul shuddered, looking around the hot, disordered

room. How much the boy must master to make sense of their tenuous poverty.

Don Raoul had developed a ledger memory for old transactions, not only his own but those recorded in the rows of Obermuller ledgers, too. He had studied the accounts all the way back to the 1730s. 'It is our history,' he said. He was fascinated with the simple statistics: the price of maize and sugar cane a century before; or the plans and costings for the irrigation of new plantings that now were old or exhausted, the land having returned to its proper desolation. Tio Alex seemed to listen deferentially but took nothing in. The ledgers that attracted him were those that related to the mine.

The thick paper of the ledger books bore a castle watermark. It was clothy in texture, rough-edged. Viewed from the fore-edge, the books were like cliffs of slate in which a child imagines fossils.

Don Raoul's years were marked by a deterioration of everything except the quality of the records. They still aspired to the permanence of chronicles.

When he placed the chronicles back on the dark shelves, he admitted that it was a struggle, triumph was no nearer. Because he was not severe with himself, he had become indulgent of what was his – not the people, but the land they lived on. He broke the old, strict rules of husbandry, entertaining hope for next year when this year failed. 'Next year, next year' was his refrain, and Tio Alex tried to believe him. They had lost hold of the present. All they had now were the blank pages of the future. Don Raoul trusted his brother with the most serious responsibility: the heir, in whom he could not quite believe.

Don Raoul had come to prefer the heavy atmosphere of his high room to the open fields. After years of riding out, of projects, he was weary. The whole house had acquired the atmosphere of a breath long held.

It was said that each Indian idol had once had, inset, a precious stone that focused its divinity, that was its life. The Spaniards killed the god by working loose the talisman, making it an amulet to wear around neck or ankle. Something less tangible, but as real, had been taken from La Encantada, from Don Raoul. Its absence at first enraged and then subdued him.

His room was filled with the extra staleness of cigar smoke. He scattered ash among the natural dust.

'Raoul, this heat will make you ill,' Tio Alex said, choking in the close atmosphere.

The high room took the full weight of the sunlight on its flat roof, through its panes that looked four ways. Don Raoul could survey his entire world from his punishing oven, and at night he stood visible above the plain, pacing to and fro or hunched at his table, surrounded by reflections of himself against the night. He never drew the curtains. A yellow calendar from the old century curled on one wall. Here the Obermullers had presided over the expansion of their world. The tide withdrew. The disorder was an inheritance, papers jumbled like memory in the embossed davenport, its drawers half-open, spilling bills, documents, parchments. It was at home with the crystal lanterns dimmed by cobwebs on the dark stairs and the crenelations on the house façade: the apotheosis of discontinuities, a Babel of hopes and styles and failures, recorded on paper or in stone.

On paper, such elegant calligraphy! Each ledger witnessed to a discipline of hand that might have won a draughtsman's praise. The plans and maps were works of art. Don Raoul had taught himself to write the way the Obermullers did, acquiring the angular, tapering style. The ledgers for 1750 and 1907 belonged to one tradition.

Unrolled on a low table lay a vast tattered map of the estates on which successive generations had drawn in their acquisitions. From two small islands of territory – El Abanico and the hacienda buildings – the property had grown to fill more than half the area. In Don Raoul's time it had ceased to grow. He had sold three parcels of land to the Lebruns, to the south. These losses were not yet marked on the map.

Father to son, father to son, the estates grew until Don Raoul bought them from the European agent of Otto Obermuller. The last Obermuller was a handsome bumpkin. He went 'back to Saxony'. *Back* to Saxony! He'd never been there in the first place! Nor had his father or grandfather. Still, the young man went home, where he'd never been, and stayed there, learning the language, covering his bare Creole roots with unfamiliar soil. Don Raoul's son was a Creole too, but he had no dreams of going home.

After five years and Paula's departure, Don Raoul had learned to envy Otto Obermuller, impulsively departing, his pockets full of money, to be free of the cane fields and the heat, of the albatross of labour, the weather's treachery, the large and little tempests of history. Did Otto now, in middle age, think back to La Encantada, its bulging windows paned with old blue glass, old as the crumbling but indestructible fabric of the house itself? Did he recall the landscapes and the Indian faces that crowded his first years, before his mother – imported, of course, from Munich – built up for him an image of his *other* home? The young man had sold up when his father was scarcely settled in his grave in the old chapel. Finding himself an orphan, how resolutely he had acted to discard the weight that fell upon him! Otto sold out for a good sum, and went to seek his future in a remoter past. It did not matter whether in Saxony he became a squire and kept his fine complexion or lost all his fortune at the gambling tables. He had gone, he had been free to go.

Don Raoul imagined Otto Obermuller: a married man, raising a family in some suburb of Berlin, or in Dresden, or with a small property beside a river, where the land was green and gentle, in winter snow fell, summers were temperate. There were large porches and the neighbours came for chocolate, cribbage. His children grew tall into their inheritance, appeared and disappeared among the pines. At night in his high, lighted room, he thought of Otto and tasted in advance the loneliness that stalked him.

'I do not speak of friends for the boy,' he repeated. 'He needs companions. He must play, run about, grow stronger. And he has to master their language. All of this –' he gestured vaguely at the room, at the world that spread below them into haze, '– all of it will be his to understand and manage.' Then, stubbing out his cigar, 'I will have Don Pepe bring boys from the village.'

7

Don Pepe on his black horse herded five young peons into the courtyard. They wore blue trousers tied with string at the waist, spotless threadbare shirts, and straw hats. Don Pepe drove them into a corner, dismounted, shrilled a command at them, and burst into the house.

'Don Alejandro!' he cried. 'Don Alejandro!'

The tutor looked down the dark stairwell at the steaming face of the overseer.

'I have brought the young peons as Don Raoul commanded!'

Tio Alex regretted the news quite as much as the boy did.

'What are we to do with them?'

Don Pepe shrugged. That was not his business. He had been told to bring them and he had brought them.

The boys stood like statues under the blind arcade, paralysed by Don Pepe's orders. They had been scrubbed and combed by their mothers, also at Don Pepe's instruction. He had not troubled to explain why they were wanted at the hacienda, how long they would be required, when they might return. Half the village had gathered in a sullen crowd to see them herded away like conscripts by the overseer.

'Come,' said Tio Alex. 'We mustn't keep them waiting.'

The boy followed, wishing he could hold Tio's hand, but thinking it better to stand alone. Don Pepe came too. He glared at the boys, then called them one by one and presented them to Tio Alex. They were instructed to call the boy *patron*.

When the introductions were over, silence fell. Tio Alex could think of nothing to do with them.

'Thank you, Don Pepe,' he said, realizing that the man's

presence did not make his task easier. 'I will look after them.'

'Shall I call back for them in an hour?'

'I think they are old enough to make their own ways home.'

The boys very nearly smiled. Don Pepe saw that he was dismissed, gave his troop a furious glance, then leapt on his horse and vanished out the side gate.

Tio Alex's first impulse was to dismiss the boys as well. Instead, he led his silent band out of the gate, following in the dust-wake of the horseman. It was better not to take them through the hall. They marched along the front of the hacienda, then down the north side, turned in among the parched rows of vegetables and yellow herbs and climbed the steps of the wide, shaded kitchen porch. The young peons kept their eyes averted, hesitating at the steps. Tio Alex urged them on. One by one they removed their hats, clutched them at their chests, and came into the shade. Tio Alex felt absurdly like a sergeant or a priest.

'Sit here.' He indicated a long bench. They sat, and the little *patron* sat with them, though they kept a distance from him.

'Marie!' Tio Alex called. 'Margarita!'

At a table used for spreading laundry, he ordered the servants to set out food: biscuits and fruit, jugs of tamarind-flavoured water. Still the boys held back, but at his order, they advanced and began eating shyly, hungrily, with their hands, until nothing was left.

Now they had feasted together, they became less constrained. Tio Alex used all his skills and they began first to walk and then gradually to run about the kitchen gardens. They were playing, and the boy was playing too, though they treated him diffidently, as if with fear. Tio Alex sat down in the shade, exhausted.

From his high room, Don Raoul caught glimpses of the native boys as they ran to the foot of the kitchen gardens, right to the chapel wall, and back again; and of his son, white hat perched askew, running among them. He rested his brow on the window-pane and watched.

Each week the boys came – five, then four, then three. At last only Isidro, the favourite, arrived, no longer driven by Don

Pepe but brought proudly by his father who passed that way to the fields or the railway halt.

Isidro and the little *patron* explored the outbuildings and ventured into the cane fields. Tio Alex let them be. So long as they said where they were going, they were free. Isidro took charge of the *patron*. He was venturesome and strong. He knew how to take advantage of the luck that had given him the run of the hacienda itself. Back in his village, he told tales of the place – the wealth of it, gold plates they ate from, rare dishes that were served, favours bestowed upon him . . . though in fact he never stepped into the house. The villagers half believed him when he came back in the evening with little gifts.

It was Isidro who taught the boy to ride a horse properly – or rather, to ride slouching and comfortable as the peons did. With Tio Alex it had been a matter of clutching the rider by the waist. But now each boy had a horse and they rode out far, sometimes to the very foot of El Abanico, where the steep broken road climbed to the summit. But Isidro refused to go up, inhibited by some superstition.

Tethering their horses to the tough cane, they swam in the canal at midday. The water was slow and thick; it filled them with lethargy. They lay on the bank for an hour or more. Always they were talking – the boy's accent became less correct, coarsened by the dialect he learned. Once a week seemed too little. They would have preferred to ride out every day. When they trotted through the deep cane like insects through a grassy field, the blades meeting high above their heads and filtering sunlight through in sequin points and narrow blades, they imagined longer expeditions. Tio Alex and the boy had read Exquemelin, the voyages of Marco Polo, and Isidro was introduced to incredible stories of distant lands and cities, and the sea. They imagined the journey to Veracruz, the train ascending to the capital and then making its gradual descent down the other side of the Cordillera to the old fortress city on the Gulf. It wound through hanging forests, scents of vanilla and jasmine, past Orizaba with its gradual skirts of volcanic spill, its cock-eyed crater with a ruff of snow, down and down towards the blue-green expanse of water that the boy knew from books, and the smell of fish and weed. Isidro and he embarked on a boat they made of canes and sisal rope and

31

turned back their eyes, surveying the coast. The land rose like El Abanico fanned open in the sun, then the haze obliterated the near shore, those mountains were suspended as on air, vanishing and vanishing until they fell away altogether and the sea was on all sides, blue and whispering like the fields of cane, but cool. There was a breeze across the deck, snapping the rag they raised as an ensign. They pictured women at the rail, wide-brimmed hats bowed in place with white scarves knotted at the chin. Europe they never reached. They stayed at sea.

It was such a journey Paula would have made when she fled from La Encantada. The boy had imagined it so often that it was entirely familiar to him. There was no detail of it that he was not able to describe to Isidro: the spectacular wilderness of the descent, those dripping cliffs, the steam that rose at dawn out of the valleys, as if from the heart of some waking volcano, and Orizaba – the name was an enchantment . . . He did not mention his mother, he could not put a face or voice to her, but he deduced her from the things she had left behind, and from the ways he invented to follow her.

8

When the rains came, they did not ride out and play in the fields. Since Isidro was forbidden the house, they played in the courtyard until the clouds piled up to the east and spread their shadows towards El Abanico. Gradually the plain vanished, first under shadow and then behind the slanting rain. Big drops spattered on the cobbles. The boys ran out through the gate and around to the kitchen porch, where they watched while the soil was churned by the violent water. Lightning burst on the mountain; sometimes a bolt hit the lightning rod on the roof of La Encantada and sputtered down into the earth; or it would strike the blackened weather vane on the unfinished chapel tower, bleaching the windows, blinding the children for whole minutes with its brightness. Such attacks of rain lasted an hour or so, then the boys went into the steaming air to explore the stables and outbuildings.

Once they went into the chapel itself.

The door was not locked, but stiff on its hinges with disuse. Inside, the air was still, with a stifling smell of bats. A bird flew out through a broken pane in the cupola. They held their breath. The door creaked to behind them. Their eyes tried to adjust to the intermittent light from the high windows that blended in a greenish atmosphere. The altar light glowed dimly like a star.

'It's like being underwater,' the little *patron* whispered. The floor was soft, carpeted with bat droppings. They advanced along the side aisle. Old pews were mossy, the wood perished; they retained their form out of habit and disuse, but to the touch they were crumbly. Better not touch. Behind a grille on the

33

south wall was a family tomb, the imperial name 'OBERMULLER' in thorny Gothic letters. A lamp hung within, *aeternum*, but extinguished, chained to the wall by dense cobwebs. '*Hic jacet*,' the boy read, '*cinis pulvis nihil*.'

'How are they buried?' asked Isidro in a husky voice. 'There is no room for more than two.'

'They dig a deep vault and pile them up.'

'How many?'

'All the Obermuller family.'

'Ten?'

'More than ten,' the boy reflected. 'More than twenty.'

Isidro clutched the rusty grille and squinted in. Stone flowers and stone foliage of an unfamiliar pattern; stone babies with wings supported a stony canopy. Bones of a rat curled in a corner, and the slightly moving veils of spider webs breathed in the breeze the boys made with their movements and their whispering.

'On the Day of Judgement, how will the ones on the bottom of the pile get out?'

'The ones above will help them, of course. They're all from the same family.'

Isidro changed the subject. 'Where will your people be buried, *patron*?' he asked.

It had never occurred to the boy that they would die – Tio Alex, Tia Thérèse, his father. He looked through the green light at the far wall. Up at the altar end, a black cross hung. In a niche, St Christopher carried a weight of guano on his back.

'Over there,' he said decisively.

'Will you put Don Alejandro there, too?'

'Certainly.'

'And Dona Thérèse?'

He paused. 'Tia Thérèse as well.'

'And you, too, in this place?'

He did not answer that. Instead, he asked: 'Where do your family get put when they're dead?'

'In the ground. There's a place near the village. But we give them flowers. They lie side by side. I have two brothers there, and aunts and uncles,' he said nonchalantly, feeling a little superior to his companion who had no bereavements to his credit. 'The priest says that on the last day the boxes will burst

34

open by themselves, and the dead will rise up singing in their white cloths.'

'What will they sing?'

'*Gloria*, I suppose.'

'Are your dead left in the weather, without a roof?'

'What sort of roof could we build for them?' asked the boy. 'Our own roofs are bad enough. We take them gifts on All Souls' and spend the night with them.' He walked up the nave to the altar. Talking gave him courage.

It was years since the host had been consecrated in the chapel – perhaps not since the boy was christened and the priest handed him in a long white gown back to his mother while the bell rang out. Yet the chapel was not a ruin. The dome and the cupola withstood the worst of the weather; it was cool. Someone kept the altar lamp lighted and swept the immediate precinct. It would not be impossible to clean the whole place up and light the lamps. Don Raoul's son fingered an old missal, damp as rag. Opening the cover, it collapsed under his hand. He crossed himself, as he had seen Margarita do.

The pulpit was of stone, and he ascended, gazing down at Isidro. Isidro was contemplating the burdened St Christopher.

'Let's clean the saint!' he said in a loud, outdoor voice, and before he could be stopped, he had climbed on to the stone bench to the icon's skirts. Reaching up cautiously, he brushed away the crumbling webs, and then with greater firmness brushed the waist, the chest, the shoulder, uncovering gilding and deep hues. But as he reached the wooden child and touched its foot, it came loose and fell forward, scattering over him the thick deposit of dust and guano. He screamed and rushed for the door, followed by his friend.

'What have you done? What have you done?'

From the door they looked back at the icon. The Christ-child had not fallen to the floor but, secured by webs and by its swaddling robe, hung upside-down against the chest of St Christopher, who feebly sparkled with gold leaf.

'You cannot leave the child like that, Isidro!'

But they left him after all and closed the door.

9

'What has happened to the young peons? Don Pepe says they no longer come to the house.'

Tio Alex had been summoned rather abruptly. His brother addressed him in a tone that reminded him of their childhood, when he had erred by commission or omission.

'One boy still comes,' he said. 'The son of Don Alegundo, the one in charge of stores at the village. The boy is called Isidro.'

'And the others?'

'They stopped coming a long time ago.'

'Why did you tell me nothing of this?'

'You have been so busy – you never asked, and I don't want to trouble you. It hardly seemed important.'

'Did you tell Don Pepe? He is angry: he thought the boys had been bad and you had sent them away, or lazy and failed to come. He wants to know what he is to do with them.'

'He is to do nothing,' said Tio Alex, a little angrily. 'He is to thank them for coming and their families for letting them come. And if he wants further information, you can refer him to me.'

Don Raoul caught the impatience in his brother's voice and changed the subject. He knew, when he paused to consider, that Don Pepe was *metiche* and resented it if the world turned without his by-your-leave. Any transactions involving the peons he felt he had the right to manage. 'I am the overseer, Don Raoul, until you no longer need me,' he had said with such a mixture of unctuousness and jealousy that the *patron* had at first been alarmed that he might give notice. Now he realized it was temperament, the prima donna approach he had come to

36

expect from those to whom he delegated any authority on the estate.

'What does the boy do with this . . . Isidro?'

'He has learned to ride. I think he knows his way around the fields now.'

'How often do they play?'

'His father brings him once a week. They have become quite friendly.'

'I told you, I do not want him to have friends – it is for exercise, to put a little muscle on him.'

'Call them companions, then. Isidro calls him *patron* or *patroncito*, which amuses me.' Don Raoul was less amused. Tio Alex continued: 'They ride out and your son is now a proper horseman. He rides with confidence, like a peon. It does me good to watch them. Sometimes,' he added, 'I wish I could still ride with him.'

'So do I,' Don Raoul said caustically, 'because he could go too far if left alone. Keep a close eye on the boy, Alex. I saw him riding towards the village yesterday and the day before, after his morning lessons. Didn't you miss him?'

'I was lying down,' his brother said.

'He did not tell you where he had gone?'

It struck Tio Alex as odd that he had not done so – but it was true. So the boy had a secret, then.

'He rode along the main path through the cane fields. Once a week! I believe he sees this Isidro every day, when you are lying down, as you say. I have a good mind to tell the priest in the village to keep *his* eye on the boy.'

'That will not be necessary. The boy and I can discuss it tomorrow, during our reading, so it will not be given too much importance.'

'He must not go to the village, Alex. He must not get too close to them. The domestic servants are another matter. They are people of trust. But he must keep a proper distance from the peons. It's not just the chance of disease, though there's always sickness in the village and you can smell it even up here sometimes. And it's not that he might get talking to them. But you know there are troubles at the coast, and now in the capital – rumours, deaths. They come uphill, they come downhill – rumour has its own logic. Things might be dangerous and I do

37

not want my son exposed.' He looked to the east as if at a dark cloud. 'A proper distance, Alex. You must teach him.'

'I am sorry. I have not been very well this year.'

A stableman led two saddled horses into the courtyard below. Isidro followed, calling *Patroncito!* It's time to go!'

'Where are they going, Alex?'

'I have no idea.'

Don Raoul heard his son's spurred footsteps on the steps outside. The front door slammed. The boys leapt on to their mounts and rode out through the side gate in a cloud of dust and laughter, cantering off down the main road to Santa Marta. Don Raoul stared after them. His son might not ride straight, like a gentleman, but he *did* ride well. That he conceded.

'Surely they are not going to the town,' he said.

'Surely not,' said Don Alex.

'They must be called back.'

'Please, Raoul. I will speak with the boy tomorrow. Let me handle the matter.'

'Keep a close eye on him then, Alex. I have trusted you with him.' Then he saw how pale his brother looked. He stubbed out his cigar and said, 'Go lie down.' Again he sensed the solitude that awaited him. It awaited each of them – his brother and his son as well.

For the rest of the day, Don Raoul kept glancing down towards the road to Santa Marta. At first it was just a reflex, to see if they were coming. Then his looking grew more urgent as afternoon passed into evening and the plain grew dark. He paced the full length of his lighted room, smoking. The clock chimed ten, eleven. Could the boy have been abducted? Don Raoul began to hate the young peon, to hate Don Pepe and the impulse that had led him to risk his child in such a way. Was the boy injured? Midnight.

Or had he fled, the boy with the mother's face, had he followed her? In his mind, the idea of injury combined with the memory of betrayal. He suffered, and he made himself suffer more, letting his mind discover a hundred explanations, each less plausible, more cruel to himself, until when two o'clock was striking he heard the sound of horses in the courtyard. He must have dozed off. They were there.

He hurried down. The boys were exhausted. They had

walked much of the way back because one of the horses had gone lame. They had ridden double, but it was slow going and Isidro's horse had tired. The stableman, awakened and grumbling, took the horses to their stalls.

'What kept you?'

'Can Isidro sleep here tonight? It's so late,' the boy said, so tired he could hardly stand. In the darkness, he could not see his father's face. He hardly heard him.

'He can go home,' the *patron* replied.

'It's so far in the dark, Papa! Let him sleep on the kitchen porch, or on the straw in the stables.'

'He can go home now, immediately.'

'Papa . . .'

But Isidro did not wait. He vanished.

'Where did he take you?'

'We went to Santa Marta.'

'Why are you so late?' Don Raoul kept the rage out of his voice, though he was suffocating with it.

The boy said, 'I'm sorry poor Isidro couldn't stay. I'm so tired, I expect he's at least half-dead.' He would have liked to lean on his father's arm, but they ascended the stairs singly. Without a 'goodnight', his father passed the second landing, climbed to his lantern room and extinguished the lights.

The boy lay on his bed for a long time, too tired to sleep, too troubled.

At first he was angry that Isidro had been sent home at such an hour and in such a way. Then, dimly at first, he began to fear the consequences. From more than a mile away, they had seen the lights in his father's high room. They were glad of the beacon and grew cheerful. Now the pleasures of the day were soured.

They *had*, it is true, lingered in Santa Marta, riding up and down the town, Isidro courting the attention of the girls. They had gone to Santa Marta before, and each time they grew more intrepid, stayed longer, dismounted and wandered in the streets. They were always amazed by the number of people that crowded through the market, by the noise, by the opulence of the civic buildings and some of the little baroque palaces along the main street, by the church with a reredos that seemed to be made of pure gold. There, the miraculous image of Our Lady of the Plains stood, swathed in silk and banked with votive candles. There, they had prayed, Isidro instructing his *patron*, and then sat for more than an hour in the plaza, under the sea-blue canopies of the jacarandas.

They had lingered, left late and, in their haste, lamed one of the horses. But they had seen so much! He would tell his father all that they had done. That would make him forget his anger. And Tio Alex would help – he always liked the stories his nephew told.

10

Early the next day Don Raoul summoned Don Pepe. The sound of his horse's hooves on the cobbles woke the boy, but he fell back into his own nightmare.

'I want Alegundo, the peon in charge of stores, to be moved from the village. Send him to El Manantial.'

El Manantial was the poorest of the villages on the estate, and the most remote, a full ten miles to the east. It was reserved for the old and those that Don Raoul, following the Obermuller practice, called 'the improvident'.

'When are they to go?' Don Pepe asked, concealing the pleasure this instruction gave him.

'Before tonight.'

Don Pepe paused. 'That peon, Alegundo, is the father of your son's friend Isidro.'

'Is he? I did not know my son had friends in the village.'

'I brought him with some others, on your instruction. He and Isidro are *cuates*, close as twins. In the village they even think Isidro is important,' said Don Pepe, making his disgust apparent.

'I know nothing of this. Alegundo and his family are to move. And if what you say is indeed the case – as I have no reason to doubt – then instruct Alegundo that his son will not be welcome at La Encantada in future.'

Don Pepe flashed a gold-toothed smile. It would be a pleasure. The favour shown to the boy Isidro had begun to worry him. Alegundo was putting on airs, and the boy told such tales. Don Pepe would perform Don Raoul's task immediately, like a genie. 'It's for the best,' the taciturn overseer allowed himself to say.

At first, the boy knew only that his punishment was not to be able to ride out again. 'We can't afford to lame another horse,' his father said. He did not listen when the boy tried to tell him of the excursion to the town. For several weeks he waited for his friend Isidro. But no friend came. Then Tio Alex told him.

And he was not under any circumstances to visit El Manantial.

'What is the reason, Tio?'

For the first time, Tio answered helplessly, 'Because your father says.'

Don Raoul kept a watch on his son. But he did not talk to him. They did not even eat together any more – Tio and the boy often went to the formal dining room at dinner, but Don Raoul was served in his high room. He pleaded business and kept his distance. And he watched. He discussed his son more frequently with Don Alex.

The boy grew sullen with everyone except his uncle.

Tio Alex was his advocate. 'If he is not to have companions from the village,' he asked, 'what companions *is* he to have?' He had disapproved of his brother's punishments: they had been peremptory, unconsidered, and Tio Alex had not been consulted. Quite as much as the boy did, he missed Isidro. And surely it was wrong to visit the sins – if they were sins – of the son upon the father? After their excursion, the boy told his tutor of his adventures. It made the sickbed, to which Don Alex retired with greater frequency, less intolerable. 'What friends *can* he have?'

'Friends of his own class.'

'Where are we to find such people here?'

That was the problem. There were only the Lebruns. Don Raoul suggested the name vaguely, tentatively.

'We have not seen them for years, except when you sold them the fields. Do they have sons? I have forgotten. Forty miles between us – and they could live in China for all we know about them.'

'We can try them,' said Don Raoul.

He wrote to old Lebrun inviting him and his family to come

for a few days. To his surprise, the old man accepted cordially. Immediately Don Raoul was filled with misgivings. 'They will see how we are growing poor.'

He resolved that they should not see.

Women were drafted in from the village. The east wing was cleaned and aired; the master rooms repainted, lamps repaired, and in two weeks that part of the house and the reception rooms had taken on an alien freshness. Don Raoul himself supervised. The prospect of guests so transformed him that he became civil, as if rehearsing his role.

'Will you act as hostess, Thérèse?' he asked the old woman, gaining admittance to her room after long negotiations through the servant Marie.

'I am not well.'

From the capital the train brought cases of cured meats, wine of a certain distinction and other provisions. The kitchens were revived, Marie and Margarita commanded a small troop of Indian women. All the vases, on the Friday of the Lebruns' arrival, were filled with flowers brought from Santa Marta and a few choice blooms from Tio Alex's balcony.

When the Lebruns' three vehicles – an enormous motor car and two carriages that followed at a distance – appeared on the Santa Marta road, Don Raoul, who had a new suit from the capital for the occasion, ran a comb through his beard and, with deliberate steps, descended to unlock and throw open the Dresden gate.

It was the first time a motor car had visited La Encantada. The peons in the fields watched with disbelief. The servants were terrified, but stood their ground like martyrs in their new uniforms.

Don Raoul had debated whether to wait at the gate itself or on the steps to the house. He chose the steps, and stood tall and distinguished, the picture of prosperous calm. Tio Alex, hunched and with a fresh handkerchief in his fist, was at his elbow in a new black-and-grey check suit. He had risked a blossom in his lapel, a crimson one. The boy stood with him. He was large for his new suit – gawky, too much wrist and ankle. One hand was plunged deep in a pocket. Tia Thérèse refused to descend. But she could not resist temptation, and now her white face appeared at a window.

43

Old Lebrun, a widower, came in the motor car with his four grandchildren. They were older than Don Raoul might have wished, and each was fashionably dressed – three girls (or young women) and a boy. They made a tight little group, exchanging looks and asides that excluded everyone strange to them. They noticed things such as the slightly archaic style in which Don Raoul dressed, and Don Alex, who had chosen a style too youthful, too casual for so twisted a figure. As for Don Raoul's son, he was inexhaustibly comical.

A few minutes later, the first Lebrun carriage entered the courtyard bringing the middle generation – three spinster daughters, no longer young, a son, his wife, a cousin. The second carriage, a modest one, brought the family servants.

The boy noticed his father's manners, how he handed the ladies down from their vehicles and paid those compliments that filled the pages of novels with such implausible charm. Don Raoul did it without effort, lapsing into an earlier manner.

Meanwhile, the large hot motor car heaved and sighed. Lebrun dismissed the chauffeur. 'Your roads are not easy on me, Don Raoul,' he said in a harsh, familiar voice. He wiped his red brow with a huge handkerchief.

Don Alex had impressed upon his nephew that he was the occasion of the festivities. The Lebrun grandchildren were marked out to be his friends and were to spend four days in his company. And yet from the first moment, even before they were introduced, he disliked them. Their world was quite complete without him. He saw no point at which he might break into it, even had he wished to do so. They whispered behind their hands. When his father told him to show them around the grounds, they kept finding the place 'so masculine': the courtyard with its distorted orange trees along the blind arcade, the kitchen garden with its parched rows of vegetables, the stable where one of the horses was still lame and the others were not much to brag about. They rode out one morning, but only a mile or two. The dust was intolerable to the Lebrun girls, and their brother insisted it would be discourteous to ride on without them.

Their own house, they said, was beside a river. Not a big river, but it flowed all year long, and there were willows. And a boat. Jacques was going to school in France next year, to

Rheims, said Madeleine, a plain, freckled girl full of conceit who, riding side-saddle, bounced dangerously up and down.

'I thought I saw a face at the window – a woman's face.'

'It is my mother's cousin,Tia Thérèse.'

'And where is your mama?'

'Dead,' the boy declared, but they knew the story.

He tried to stay with his father. The women's presence quite transformed Don Raoul. Even his body had a more considered movement, his voice lost its coarseness and he smiled most of the time, watching for advantage, for development. He seemed glad to have his son at his elbow. 'He rides like an Indian. Don't you, boy?' he would say. Or he asked Tio Alex, 'How is your scholar doing?' and Tio Alex would report in too much detail on the progress of their studies. Old Lebrun seemed to like the boy, but the young members of his party looked away. He was so gauche, he stuck out of his clothes as though they had shrunk on him.

On the last evening, the great dining room was transformed. The ghost put on flesh one final time, Don Alex said. The mirrors that lined the walls, the crystal lamps that twinned with their reflections, had been polished. Huge bowls of flowers scented the air – it was almost a garden. The table was an acre of mahogany polished until it glowed like a dance-floor by candlelight, the napkins folded upright like girls in starched dresses; the seals on the wine-bottles were insignia worn by formal gentlemen. Because the visit was coming to an end, everyone relaxed into the evening. The boy was proud that his father could entertain in this fashion, and remembered that he was himself the occasion.

These pale people, who resembled relations and spoke French with a stiff correctness, as though they had learned it from books – why had they not made more of one another? They had been as good as neighbours for sixteen or seventeen years, yet only Don Raoul and old Lebrun had met before, and then for business. In future, their families would meet often. This dinner marked the end of a visit, perhaps, but the beginning of something larger.

They were dazzled by the candlelight thrown back by the mirrors, by the room multiplied into a hundred rooms. It was hot and rich with the smell of food, flowers, cigar smoke, the

45

fumes of wine. It dissolved outward in its reflections, the place was an open plain, and the people in it a nation set down specially for the pleasure of the night. There should have been dancing. Don Raoul was larger than a host: he was a king, elegant and benignly moving among them.

But his son was not quite a prince. Not yet. Don Raoul courted old Lebrun. Perhaps a granddaughter would be eligible, would become eligible. A dream – the entertainment stirred such dreams: the two estates, La Encantada and the Lebrun's, might marry in the son and a granddaughter. Lebrun's fortune had grown at Don Raoul's expense. One ceremony would recover all.

But Lebrun was at best curious. When Tio Alex talked to him about the disused mine, the old man began to sense that beneath the hospitality lay a hunger, a poverty that chilled him. The Obermullers, intolerable Prussians though they were, had been better at the land than the eccentric host and his relations.

Still, the old house was full of laughter and of music snatched casually from old instruments. Don Raoul watched the women with a cruel intensity.

Very briefly Dona Thérèse appeared among them, startling the girls. ('It's the ghost!' Madeleine exclaimed behind her hand.) She moved with dignity in her black dress. 'It is not truly peaceful here,' she said to old Lebrun. 'There are the birds with their terrible morning noises!' She disappeared before Don Raoul could present her to the ladies, but he took her appearance as a good omen. Things might return to normal. All doors were not yet closed.

When the Dresden gate was locked behind the guests next day, Don Raoul climbed to his room. By evening he had counted the cost of the entertainment and had subsided into himself once more. The flowers were removed, the drawing rooms were closed. The boy, his father and uncle dined together in the mirror room, but there was no residue of magic there and their silence dilated through the house. That room too, Don Raoul ordered, should be closed.

Don Alex insisted that it had been a great success. But the visit was not returned. A few months later they learned that the Lebruns had gone to France, leaving their estates in the charge of a major-domo and an agent.

46

'They're back in Paris. I suppose they keep two motor cars now,' said Tio Alex, thinking of the streets where they would live, their leisure, the loved places they would see for the first time, which he would not see again.

'They were always a step or two ahead,' Don Raoul said, as if it did not matter to him. His troubles were gathering.

11

Don Raoul watched his brother closely. Week by week he dwindled. It caused him almost physical pain to hear his brother breathing, to see him hunch over his illness, trying to suppress a cough. Yet Alex would not surrender his task of tutor. It was the thing he lived for: to teach his nephew and, should he live long enough, to reconcile him with his father.

But Don Raoul believed he needed rest and he looked for ways of lightening the responsibility of teaching. He must do it tactfully. He must prolong that life which had come to mean so much to him at La Encantada. It was for his own sake that he wanted Alex to live.

For the first time in years, Don Raoul thought of the Church. The idea startled him with its simple rightness. The boy's spiritual education had been overlooked entirely. Alex was a secular creature, despite the threat of an early religious vocation. As for Don Raoul, he did not believe, he did not pray, the issue never entered his mind, which was too busy with the problems of the day.

'The boy must be catechized and confirmed, Alex. What is the priest from the village like? You used to call him an intellectual.'

'He spends his time reading novels in the patio of his house. I called him intellectual only because he reads.'

'Could he come one or two days a week to catechize?'

'I can catechize,' said Tio Alex, suddenly jealous.

'You are not a believer.'

'You hardly set an example yourself. When were you last in church?'

48

'When I was married,' Don Raoul replied. 'No,' he corrected himself, 'it was when the boy was christened.'

'I remember what it was like to believe.' Tio Alex was too much of an ironist to confess a faith, even as he was dying. But he had once believed ardently, and the order of worship filled him with exquisite nostalgia. His adolescent faith had ripened at a time when his disease seemed ennobling; he was chosen, heaven would claim him early, even before his brother and sisters, whose health would keep them labouring in the vineyard to the very latest hour. He toyed with the priestly vocation – more than toyed. His instructor was a Jesuit, and even after he abandoned his plans, his instructor came to him once a week for the pleasure of good hospitality and conversation. They continued meeting until his scepticism became intolerant.

Without conviction, but with enthusiasm, he would undertake the boy's preparation. 'The village priest is a lazy fellow. Leave the boy to me.'

His brother was reluctant, but Tio Alex pleaded with such urgency that at last he agreed.

'I can pretend that I believe, just as I pretend I do not believe.'

When the boy was ready – in two or three months at most – they would send him into retreat for a few weeks, across the plain and beyond Santa Marta, in the hills to the south. The centuries-old Augustinian monastery of San Mateo was noted for its severity and it catered to the better class of spiritual candidates. The boy could be confessed there and make his first Communion.

Tio Alex took his new responsibilities with oppressive seriousness. Weakened almost to a whisper by his illness, he struggled to make clear the points of faith, as if to redefine them for himself. Each afternoon he got out of bed, putting on his wool dressing-gown, for despite the heat he could not get warm.

'Pretend I am a monk,' he said, wearing his rough habit over his nightshirt.

He and the boy now shared the large room that had belonged to Paula and then had become the stately nursery – a room of books, full of dainty furniture and china, into opposite ends of which two beds had been fitted. On the balcony, or at the large table where the boy had learned to write, they spread black books with tongues of purple ribbon. Tio Alex had the boy look up passages in the gospels, compare them with the Prophets, then turn to works by the Church fathers. He had brought all his books with him when he came, even the texts of his discarded faith, and gradually they were resurrected from the crates and shelves in his old room and found their way on to the crowded shelves where Paula's library was. Her books were novels, collected letters, memoirs and poetry for the most part, but among them were her missal and some edifying lives of saints, like sullen novels.

Beneath his habitual cynicism, Alex discovered that he had forgotten little of what he had taken to heart in the intense sincerity of adolescence. Whole sentences of texts he had not read for years came back to him. Each morning, as he lay shivering in his bed, he read in order to prepare his afternoon lessons. Sometimes the boy read to him.

The boy might have been bored, but Tio Alex was telling him the story of his life. They had become the same age, for the years of his faith had been his teens, and he regained that youthful fervour. His disease brought back that early vulnerability. He surprised himself with the suspicion that he might believe once more. The *quia impossibile* no longer made him smile.

They hurried through their instruction. The boy's mind sometimes clouded. When the Bishop consoled Augustine's mother with the words, 'The son of your tears shall not perish,' Tio Alex could take him no further that day. Other times the boy questioned him or quarrelled, showing a settled cynicism learned from his uncle in more casual times.

'If we worship wrongly, is our sacrifice to the rebellious angels?' he confronted Tio Alex with St Augustine's question. He was troubled by the Church's claim to authority – arbitrary, like the power of a parent over a child. Earlier, when they had studied history, Tio Alex had made much of the dark deeds of the Church. They had shared the brilliant fatuities of Voltaire.

'You have become a riddle to yourself.'

'No, Tio Alex – *you* have become a riddle to me.'

'You will discover much, once you have the tools to explore yourself. Accept the tools. They have served others well.'

'And you, Tio?'

'They have not served me. Because I had forgotten them. It's late for me to start, but if I lived now I would use them.'

He was growing inward, he seldom laughed (it hurt his chest). He had become earnest, not in the resigned way that old men do, but a hectic, emphatic, youthful earnestness. On the occasions when he felt well enough to dress, he chose sombre clothes, abandoning cravats, checks and waistcoats, as if donning the habit of a priest. In his pocket he carried the missal. Had illness changed him so much, or had he sensed the boy was changing and needed a different kind of master?

For the boy was different. When Tio Alex had spoken to him of Don Raoul in the past, it had seemed to frighten him. Now he grew insolent at the mention of his father. Don Raoul was preparing to welcome him into his high room; he had told Tio Alex that after the retreat, he would begin to take his son as a partner in the estate. Even as the father softened, the son grew hard against him. Tio Alex was too exhausted to puzzle out a strategy to keep them at peace, to bring them together.

His death was not far off. Twenty-five years before, he would have welcomed it – he was 'ready for his wings', as he had told his Jesuit instructor. But the delay had robbed him of readiness. He was not in love with life, but he was attached to his nephew and even, as it began to recede, to the cruel landscape that spread beyond the windows.

He hurried the boy's instruction, but it was partly for himself that he hurried. The boy kept placing hurdles in his path, posing hard questions about dogma. He would get over them, then the boy would ask, 'Why does my father not take the Host?'

'You must ask him.'

'I cannot speak to him.'

'Then you must try.'

'And why do you avoid the Host, Tio Alex?'

'There is no priest to go to.'

'There is a priest in the village.'

'It's too late for me.' But he would ask for the priest, as soon as the boy was sent on his retreat to San Mateo. The little priest who ministered to the peons, who had been unacceptable as a spiritual instructor for his nephew, would come to him, take his confession and give him the Host. He would anoint him when the time came and say the words when he was buried. The thought consoled him: to confess after all those years of silence and inaction! He could feel grace on the threshold. Soon he would admit it.

The boy learned the answers to the usual questions. He did not believe them but he wished to please his uncle. He declared himself ready to be sent to San Mateo.

'I wish I could come with you.' But he would not leave the house again. 'If you can, understand the brothers. They are strange men – not like the Jesuits, I'm afraid. But a few of them will be wise. One or two of them may even be good.' He made a wry face. 'I would have been a good shepherd for you there. Next time, perhaps.'

Two weeks later, the rusty old carriage was got ready, and before his uncle woke, the boy set out alone for the retreat. It was further than he had ever gone, beyond Santa Marta, to the distant blue hills and the ancient house.

12

It was the same carriage in which he and Tio Alex had travelled to the foot of El Abanico more than seven years before. It had hardly been used since that time. The driver swept and dusted it but it was too far gone to take polish. It jolted along the road with none of the enchantment it had had that dark morning of their excursion.

And he was quite alone for the first time, passing the fields he and Isidro had cantered past two years ago, chasing each other, exploring the side paths. The landscape had become flat and dull, with here and there broken adobe walls where people no longer lived, their hedges of organ cactuses still fencing off their claims to privacy, the enclosures where their animals had bred. It seemed a long way to Santa Marta. He found it troubling: so many little ruins, so many abandoned lives. How much of the dust that unfurled behind the carriage, finding its way in through the cracks and the ill-fitting windows, was the dust of animals and men? In sceptical times, his uncle told him that every coin in this country had passed at least three times through the Church collection plates and boxes. What of the dust? the boy thought: how often had it breathed and walked and subsided back into itself? It was the Obermuller epitaph: *cinis pulvis nihil.*

Santa Marta was not as he remembered it. Nothing but dogs and old men seemed alive there. The carriage clattered down the main street and a few faces turned, a few dogs barked. The coachman sat sullen on his box. Beyond the town there was the same brown landscape.

In the middle of nowhere, just as he was dozing off, they lurched to a stop. He jumped down and found they were at a small inn.

'It's the only place you'll get a bite to eat before we start the climb to San Mateo,' the coachman said. He placed his fists on his hips and awaited instructions.

'We'll stop for half an hour,' the boy said.

The coachman held aside the curtain that served as a door and they stepped into a room dimly lit with tapers. A wood fire added to the stifling heat. There were low tables and men drinking pulque made from the maguey cactuses – fresh and sickly it tasted. The boy only sipped his drink. They brought chorrizo sausages that he could not touch, they smelled so strange. 'Horsemeat,' the coachman said. The bread was sandy and the corncakes half cob.

'Who's the blond boy?' one of the dark-faced drinkers asked the coachman.

'From beyond Santa Marta.'

'Where're you going?'

'To the brothers at San Mateo.'

The drinkers eyed them.

'That your carriage out there?'

The coachman did not reply.

'Hard times, it looks like. You want to sell your horses? They'd make good shoes.'

'You want to hold your tongue?' the coachman said.

'Hey, you come in here, sit down among us, and when we start to talk, you get all prickly.'

The drinkers moved towards them slowly. The boy remained silent while the coachman drank quietly, apparently unperturbed.

'If you ask me, these two are uncivil.'

'Uncivil, yes.'

'What have you got to say, boy?'

The boy stood up. He was tall – taller than the men surrounding him. He was dressed differently, too, in the formal suit he had got for the Lebruns' visit, which Margarita had let out, so it almost fitted him. He moved towards the men and they divided to let him through. He went towards the cooking fire where the innkeeper watched uneasily.

54

He thought he would complain. But there was a look of unease on the innkeeper's face.

'Buy them a drink,' he whispered. The boy understood.

'Please give each of these men a drink. I will pay.'

They left the coachman drinking, eating his chorrizo and his bread, and gathered around the foreign boy. They drank his health and started laughing. They touched his clothes.

'You don't carry a pistol,' one of them said.

'Or a machete or knife.'

'How much did these clothes cost you?'

He stood silently among them, a neutral look on his face, and when they had drunk his health a third time, he paid and made his way to the door. The coachman followed him. How fresh the air seemed, for all the heat and dust! If they could get away now . . .

They climbed aboard the vehicle and calmly set out, leaving the semi-circle of shining faces. When they had gone a hundred yards they heard a cry and one of the men shot a pistol in the air. The coachman whipped the horses and they began to speed towards the foothills. It was only a single shot, aimed into the air – a little gesture.

The boy began to feel chilly. At first he thought it was fear; he had broken out in a sweat. Then he saw that they were on rising ground, the road had begun to curve into the foothills and then to climb steeply. Scrub and mesquite became more dense, then small trees – pirul and oak. Then sun-stunted pine trees and fir, taller and fuller as they climbed into the blue hills that he had once seen as a dream landscape from the top of El Abanico. How far they were from home! Evening was falling.

13

The carriage put him down at the treble-arched gateway of San Mateo. Beyond the churchyard, the broad, plain façade of the building was in shadow. An old man appeared and carried his bags between laurels and oleanders, skirting graves and a huge amate tree. Drooping, trumpet-shaped florifundios emitted a heavy scent. Blue-green fireflies flared here and there, showing the depth of foliage.

Eden. The old man who led him did not answer questions. Was he deaf or under a vow of silence? He struggled under the luggage and the boy asked himself why he had brought so much with him into this ascetic world. But was it so much? Clothing, books, boots, his mother's writing set that Tio Alex insisted he should take, so that he could write regular letters about his progress.

They stepped through a dark arch into the first cloister.

The old man did not pause, though the boy paused to take in what he could of the fiered arches that rose above the height of the tall cypresses in the courtyard. Shadows moved among them, eyes followed him as he crossed by the fountain whose jets of water made a cross. He was led past the refectory – the smell of dinner reminded him how hungry he was – into a second cloister of more recent date, on a monumental scale, with Corinthian pilasters and a formal garden spread out from a statue of the Mother of God. The old man struggled on like a burdened ant, puffing, but without pause, to the third cloister, which was intimate, like the patio of a large house. They climbed the open stairs to the second floor. The porter threw open a small door and pointed the boy inside, then vanished.

He stepped into the dark. He fumbled for the crack of evening light at the shutters, found the latch and threw them open. A tide of cool air and winged insects filled his narrow room. A window-seat was set into the thick wall. There he might read by daylight and gaze out at the hills. A trestle bed with a straw-filled mattress – the kind they had for the servants at La Encantada – ran along one side. A plain table and chair and two hooks for his clothing completed the cell. For company, over his bed hung a simple crucifix of great delicacy, the figure of Christ carved in ivory, and even in the dimness the fine veins were like wounds on the bowed figure.

There was a candle on the table but no means of lighting it. He settled on the bed and covered his eyes with his hands. From no clear direction came the sound of chanting – not music, exactly, but a kind of undertone. He felt tired and – in a way he had not sensed before – safe, as though he had shed himself, La Encantada, his father, his growing rage of disenchantment. Perhaps he had come to the right place. If only he knew where to wash his hands and face . . .

When he awoke, a tall man in a robe stood over him. He had a rope knotted at his waist and large, soft hands crossed on his belly.

'It is time for supper.'

The boy rose up dazed and, still in his travelling clothes, followed the figure into this new world of shadow and denial.

'You are from La Encantada, I think.'

'Yes, Father.'

'What sort of place is it?'

'Poor, dry, a sad sort of place.'

His guide changed the subject.

'There are several others on retreat here, but they are all much older than you. This is your first time here?'

'Yes, Father.'

'I am new here myself – only two years!'

They were passing a trough in the second cloister through which clear water ran.

'Might I wash my face?'

'Haven't you washed since your arrival? What is old Alegundo up to! What sort of hospitality is this!' He stopped before the trough, offered the boy a cup and a cloth, and watched him douse his face and wet his wrists up to the cuffs.

'It is an important time for you.' He added, 'They call me Brother Javier.'

'Yes, Father.'

At the door of the refectory he took the boy by the elbow and led him to his place at a long table. There was little room. He found himself half-buried between brothers and others like himself on retreat. He was introduced to each in turn. They nodded towards him with their eyes averted, their jaws working methodically. Above the sounds of eating, a voice read in a monotonous tone from the Scriptures. The dinner was almost lavish. There was wine. It went on for a long time and the boy glowed with exhaustion. Then all at once, at a signal he did not see, heads bowed, a blessing was intoned, a hearty 'Amen', and the brothers rose, processing two by two out of the room. The boy followed, having lost Brother Javier.

Because he could not see their legs, they seemed to him to glide to the cloistered entrance of the church. The doors burst open and at once they started chanting, filling the domed structure with their voices. The boy was dazzled by the light of candles reflected in the gold retables. Life-sized statues of Christ at the Stations of the Cross, with no detail of suffering omitted, and gilded saints in agony and exaltation, looked on. He knelt with the other visitors in the congregation, on the Gospel side, and tried to listen.

In the choir he eventually distinguished Brother Javier. The faces of the regular inmates, rising out of their rough-textured habits, were so nearly alike, as though their vows effaced them: they gave voice, they bent in prayer, they rose to praise. Only their ages showed, their remoteness from or proximity to the grave. Imitating their gestures, crossing himself, genuflecting, he participated in their strangeness. In contrast with the brothers, those in the pews where he knelt were various – well-dressed, pomaded, rapt in their devotion, but sometimes whispering familiarly to one another.

When the service ended, Brother Javier glided down to the boy and led him back to his cell and lighted his candle. Just as the boy prepared to say goodnight, the Brother sat down on his bed and began talking. The boy retreated to the window-seat.

'I am not your confessor. That will be Father Ignatius. I am your guide.'

'My guide?' the boy repeated, hoping that his spiritual exercises might involve some pilgrimage.

'Only through the catechism and the services!' Brother Javier said with a hoarse laugh. Then he focused a confiding look on the boy. 'Did they send you, or did you ask to come?'

'It was part of the preparation.'

'Do you think you have . . .' he paused. 'Do you think you have a vocation?'

'A vocation?'

'Do you wish to go back into the world?'

'I have hardly been in it,' the boy said, puzzled. 'I don't feel that I *have* been in it yet.'

'La Encantada is so isolated?'

'No,' he answered, 'but it is possible to live there out of sight. My uncle is my companion.'

'No friends?'

'I did have a friend . . .'

Brother Javier's face kept moving between a blank smile and a frown, like the face of a baby discomforted by wind.

'What do you think of San Mateo?'

The boy did not answer. He had formed no impression. He was dazzled, confused, and suddenly not happy.

'It is too early to ask,' Brother Javier said apologetically. 'I am sorry, only it seems to me that you are the kind of boy who might think – but it is too early still. And yet – yes, boy, keep the idea of a vocation in your mind these coming weeks. Pray for guidance. You might find yourself among us.'

Brother Javier rose slowly to his feet, placed a hand firmly on the boy's head, and blessed him. Then he left the room.

Keep the idea of a vocation in your mind. The words filled the stillness of the cell. Was he suggesting that he might stay by choice in such a place, don the rough fabric and the knotted rope? A breeze filtering through the open shutter fretted the candle flame.

Why had he come at all? The prospect of a month with this guide filled with him unease. He had not chosen him. He would write to Tio Alex!

But when the paper was before him, he did not know what to

set down. He counted the days – twenty-seven – that stretched before him, and then the carriage would take him back to La Encantada. The ivory Christ held its face slightly averted, the candlelight heightening its punishment. When the boy lay down on his bed, he was wide awake. 'I shall not sleep at all!' he said aloud. His eyes closed and he slept.

14

When Brother Javier tested him on the catechism, he answered correctly on all points.

'You have not lacked instruction.'

But the boy did not question his guide. He endured him. With Tio Alex he argued and disagreed, but to argue with Brother Javier would have been to prolong the unpleasant lessons.

Three times a day he propelled the boy to church by the elbow, steering him through his devotions. After the second Mass on his first Sunday, he was suddenly left alone. A period of private meditation was recommended.

He went out of the cloisters into the wide churchyard. It was like a prisoner's reprieve, to stand there in the world, without cloister arches, without monitory saints. How homesick he was, absurdly homesick for – La Encantada.

The huge amate tree shaded almost the whole burial ground, keeping the worst of the sun from the ranks of graves. Every kind of flower and fruit grew there, as if casually, unplanned: the lolling purple hearts of banana palms, and dates; climbing calabashes, hibiscus, roses; nasturtiums, verbena, and pert, upright papayas – Eden's profusion among flat gravestones.

At midday the Indians crowded in, kneeling at the open chapel to the left of the main church, for the people's Mass. At the corner chapels with their wreathes and chains of fresh flowers, the Host was displayed, and in procession the saints' images were borne on holy days. The boy found a recess in the trunk of the amate tree and watched the worshippers as if from a cave.

61

Gathered in the sun before the chapel, they obeyed the priest as an army obeys its commander, unhesitating, calling the responses by reflex. In a way he admired how the Augustinians trained their flock. It had no will but their own; it moved freely within the boundaries they made.

How raw the bare upturned soles of all those kneeling Indians looked, raw and dusty, as they clutched their hats at their chests, or as the women said the *Ave*, some with infants slung in their shawls, giving suck during the *Peccavi*. This removed them briefly from their daily lives. The public confession, then twice a year at the little grille inside the great church, the whispered details of lives too insignificant to trouble God, and yet given a brief importance by the dark smoke-scented space, the little candles at the Virgin's feet. In knotted handkerchiefs or in the leather scabbards where they carried their machetes, they always had a coin reserved for her.

The slow days passed. The boy came to resent the pale, mournfully smiling madonnas that stood in various costumes in the niches in the church and cloisters. Sometimes at night an enamelled eye would catch a glint of moonlight and seem to watch him walking aimlessly from terrace to terrace. The madonnas haunted him, but most of all the statue in the centre of the second cloister patio, the marble woman who was the axis of the place, surrounded by two hundred sallow men. She looked familiar, coquettish. Her mournfulness was studied, affected, unreal. Mother of God.

He wrote a long letter to his uncle.

He had a rosary of olive wood. He carried it tight in his fist. Tio Alex said it was a gift to Paula that she had abandoned with her missal and other spiritual properties when she left.

'Did she not need it?'

'Most of all when she left it in her room.'

He had her writing set and her rosary.

Brother Javier told him, 'Each day the Carmelites take a handful of earth out of what will be their graves. Each day – so that when God takes them, they will have a bed to lie in.

'Our brothers the Franciscans wear rough shirts beneath their habits and some use flails on their own backs.'

All this the boy wrote to Tio Alex. And one night a special penance was arranged for those on spiritual retreat. After midnight prayers, the candles in the church were extinguished. Into the darkness came stage-devils bearing torches – a pasteboard-and-pitch premonition of damnation. Those who could run were compelled to flee back and forth through the aisles, pursued by fallen angels with hideous faces. Some were genuinely frightened. Those who had been before played their parts solemnly. The boy hid in a confessional and watched, wondering when, between prayers and penances, the faceless brothers had found time to make such masks and practise their cautionary ritual. It ended with the timely arrival of a Christ accompanied by anthems and torches. He purged the demons. The congregation filed out and went to bed.

The prayers, hymns and chanting, the hours of solitude and of instruction, became almost intolerable. When Brother Javier entered his room, sat on his bed and cornered the boy on the window-seat, it was an act of will not to flee.

As the voice of his guide droned, he gazed out of the window, not probing his soul but watching the neighbouring fields and the Indians working. They were there with the sunrise, even before the first prayers, and their noise woke him. When the sun set, they were still there, and only at dark did they go home to the village. At first he watched them casually as a distraction, then more intently, puzzled that the same men – they looked more sturdy and prosperous than those at La Encantada – should come each day to the same field and bend over the soil with hoe and mattock. It was like that at home, but there the cane was deep and concealed the labourers.

'Could we not meet together in the library? I should like to see it.'

'I am sorry. The library is not for visitors.'

He turned the pages of his missal, Bible and other books he had brought, reading snatches here and there. Brother Javier brought edifying texts. The time for his confession was approaching.

It troubled him. Tio Alex would have seen the difficulty. But Brother Javier, who demanded confidences, he could not talk to. 'What am I to say?' he would begin, and his guide started questioning him in ways he did not understand. What were the desires, the deeds so obliquely described?

Three days before the ceremony, he was taken to meet his

confessor, a large man with heavy eyebrows who breathed as if reluctantly and spoke a few words without looking at the boy.

Striving daily with his uncle's 'spiritual tools' to sound his soul, he grew more and more puzzled. He did not know what to look for. He was not sure where to look. Had he sinned?

It occurred to him that he had done and thought nothing for himself. He was at the end of his fifteenth year and in all that time he had been governed, directed. What will had he exercised? If he had sinned, it had been his father's sins, his uncle's. He did not know what they were. He had not chosen them. To Tia Thérèse, he was a daughter, and to Tio Alex, a distraction from despair, to be played with as a cat plays with a mouse. His father gave orders and deprived him of what might have been his own. Now Brother Javier wished a vocation upon him; he was a guide who took him yet further from himself.

In the last days he grew wilful, refusing to go to church more than once a day. Brother Javier took his reticence for further evidence of moral delicacy. He confided to the confessor that here was a boy ripe for the order, undergoing serious spiritual self-questioning. He longed to have a new recruit to his credit.

The boy's mind settled on one subject – his mother, whose absence seemed now to constitute his soul. He puzzled over her desertion. He could find only one way to understand it.

It was an intuition that flowed from his resentment: his father had driven her off. By neglect or unrecorded cruelty. Tio Alex knew. He must tell the boy. There was a secret in her departure. He wrote long letters to his uncle every day, full of hypotheses, full of questions.

As he revolved it in his mind, his intuition became a certainty. He wanted to return immediately to La Encantada, to demand an answer. Her face, seen among Tia Thérèse's photographs and only half-remembered, came back to him clearly now: the lips and eyes, the even skin, the eyebrows slightly raised. Even in dreams she appeared, speaking to him; her lips moved, but he could not hear her.

Automatically at first, and then with fervour, he started to repeat the words of the *Ave*.

15

The broad flat cloister roofs, surrounded by a balustrade, served as a promenade for the guests of San Mateo. From there the boy could see El Abanico to the north reduced by distance to a mere blur. He often gazed in that direction. Tio had deceived him – or been deceived. Here the boy had met no wise or good men. He had met hardly anyone. He had learned no more than what Tio Alex had taught him, and only his doubts were clearer.

He looked from the cool hillside to the hot plain with that homesickness that had so surprised him. There were times before when he had been angry or unhappy, but never before with such concentration, without comfort or relief. He could see the life that lay in store for him: La Encantada would be his and would dwindle. Before he had begun, he had the pain of failure.

Preparing for his confession was the wryest ordeal. He studied the list of sins, what Brother Javier called the 'prompt book'. When he asked his guide to interpret the code, he refused. The older visitors on retreat came with a burden of faith settled by rote, with worldliness, age and wealth. They knew how they had sinned and how to tell on themselves. He did not talk to them beyond a solemn morning greeting or, on the rooftop promenade, a brief acknowledgement. Among so many men he felt more solitary than if he had stood alone at the summit of El Abanico, with only iguanas and birds.

The evening of his confession was at hand. He was full of joy because the next morning, his sixteenth birthday, after taking his first Communion, he would be called for – the carriage would take him home.

Brother Javier came to say goodbye.

'I will wave you off in the morning, but I wanted a last word.'

He clutched the boy's hand and would not let it go.

'Shall we see you here again, for a longer stay?'

He stood silently looking at the boy's blank face. Then he placed both hands on his head and said a prayer and blessing that seemed interminable. Suddenly he kissed him on both cheeks and left the cell. It was as though a mist had lifted: Brother Javier departed from his life. His gaoler was gone. The scent of freedom was in his nostrils.

After the evening service, the boy entered the church with a light heart. There were others lined up on either side of the confession box, waiting their turn, some in silent prayer, some standing vacantly. The dark leather curtain was drawn across in front of the priest. His sandals showed, and a fold or two of cassock. The toes moved from time to time reflectively.

The boy stood at the foot of a life-sized madonna. He gazed up at her. She gazed at the vault. On her hand, slightly raised, sat a blue-swaddled infant, his bare little feet quite white in the candle light, his dimpled wrist and elbow reaching out. For a moment the boy loved the woman with exceptional tenderness. Then he was called.

He advanced to the left and knelt at the dark grille.

He heard the priest's troubled breathing. It was like visiting a sick man and tasting the air of his confinement. He said the *Pater Noster*, crossed himself, and then in a choked whisper the words came out, so muted that they seemed to rise from a great depth, as if the Baptist's voice were sounding from the well. At first, the confessor did not take his meaning.

'What did you say, my son?'

The boy spoke more decisively. 'Father, I have not sinned.'

There was a pause in the dark breathing, then a gathering sound. 'Not in thought?'

'Not in thought.'

'Not in word?'

'No.'

'Not in action?'

'No.'

'Then you are indeed in sin.' The boy held his breath to learn

66

what he had done. 'You have lied to yourself, and to God. Or you are thick with pride,' the priest declared with a vehemence that must have made his judgement audible to those who waited their turn. 'Every man has sinned. You have been here four weeks to find your sin, to prepare yourself for first Communion. Come, my son, you must have found some sin in yourself.'

'I could not find any, Father. I looked. I checked against the list.'

'Then you are blind. You should not trouble me with this. There are others waiting, serious men.'

'You told me to come.'

'And for your trouble, boy, I give your pride a penance. Say to yourself, phrase by phrase, the *Peccavi*, and in each phrase discover yourself as you are.'

'Yes, Father.' After a pause. 'Your blessing, Father?'

'No!' he exclaimed, and clicked closed the little shutter on the grille. The boy could hear him shift his bulk to the other haunch, open the other shutter, and the conventional whispering began again.

He came out into the dazzling candlelight, the fresher air of incense, and went slowly towards the door and cloister, keeping his eyes averted from the saints and toiling Christs. He was heavy with his innocence – as if guilty of it. Yet in the boredom and effort of his retreat he had not found sin. The sin would have been to lie, to invent misdeeds. If only he had some true thing to confess! The silly verses of Tia Thérèse's ballad came back to him:

> *One boy marched behind*
> *And two boys marched before.*

The air of the open cloister broke over him, cold and starlit, and the fountain made its cross of water beyond the foliage of the jasmines. It was too cold now for the scent of flowers. Everything in the shadows was withheld with the blessing. He went back to his cell where the candle burned. His missal flickered, as if with its own light, open at the list of sins he had yet to commit. He wanted to slam the book, make a noise like whiplash, break the spell of a place so sunken in its calm it

67

might have been three fathoms under water, under ground. But his hand was tame. It drew the ribbon marker down, it smoothed the pages and closed the book.

He blew out the candle, moved to the window and opened the shutters. For an instant the madonna seemed to stand there, with the infant; then there was only moonlight. He let himself cry.

He was waiting for the carriage at the triple-arched gate of the churchyard when the clock struck seven. The same little silent man had fetched his luggage, set it down and disappeared. First Mass had been said, but the boy had missed it. Brother Javier did not wave him off.

The boy had travelled to the blue hills for a tedious dream; it troubled him beyond waking.

16

The courtyard was strewn with straw. It was a city custom, but
Don Raoul could think of no other gesture to ease his brother
and soothe his own sense of helplessness. He had them spread
the best straw from the stables. He whispered hoarsely to his
brother, 'The courtyard will be quiet. I have had them scatter
straw so you can sleep.' His brother's lips smiled but his eyes
did not open. He loved Raoul very simply now, the way he did
as a boy when Raoul was his protector, when he sat beside his
bed during his first convalescence and told him about Paris.

Don Raoul was in and out, in and out, fretful for the boy's
return.

'When he gets back, he will nurse you back to health. I
cannot spare you, Alex. *He* cannot spare you. You'll see – in no
time now, you'll be sitting at the window again. Then – we'll
take it step by step – the balcony, the courtyard. If we take it
easily . . .' He almost believed what he was saying. 'Remember
how it was the first time. We were younger then, I know, but it
was as bad as this and it passed.'

But Alex grew worse.

'I will get the doctor to come from Santa Marta if you like.'

The carriage arrived after dark. Don Raoul himself opened
the Dresden gate to the boy. His son hardly acknowledged the
greeting. He was looking up towards the room he shared with
Tio Alex. Only a vague candle burned there, and as the
carriage moved over the cobbles, it made so little sound –
unreal, as though it moved on air. His father helped him down
and set his lips to the boy's cheeks. He embraced him. The boy
decided it was indeed a dream.

'Tio is unwell,' his father whispered.

'I will go to him,' the boy said, running towards the door.

'Not now, son. Come to my room and I will tell you.'

'He is dead!'

'No.' Then, 'Not yet.'

They climbed in silence to the top of the house. Below, the servants were carrying in the boy's things from the carriage. He brought back precisely what he had taken, nothing more.

One of the horses whinnied in harness. Evening chilled its sweated sides. The team had fairly flown along the last miles, having caught scent of the stable.

Don Raoul closed the door of the lantern room. It had grown strange to the boy and he gazed at the window where his reflection moved on the wide night beside his father's. They were the same height now – one slender and alert, the other heavy-set, ballasted with failure.

The disorder of the room contrasted with the stiff orderliness of San Mateo. Yet here too was a kind of austerity, every object a concentrated symbol, a memento.

'Your uncle is very ill. He will not live.'

But I must have my question, the boy thought. His first feeling was not sorrow but urgency. Sorrow would come later. He needed now to shake the invalid awake and get his answers quickly, while there was enough breath. Tio alone could make matters clear.

It did not occur to him that his father might tell him what he wanted. He did not know how to address him, the remote watcher, the depriver. Yet they stood together in the lantern room confronting the same loss.

Don Raoul poured two glasses of amber wine. '*Salud*,' he said, and they drank the warming liquid. 'Have you eaten?'

'Something. We did not stop. I brought some bread from San Mateo.'

'How was it?'

The boy shrugged.

Then, helplessly, his father said, 'What shall we do?'

'What *can* we do?'

'And Thérèse, it will kill her.'

The boy looked up.

70

'She is watching. Her ear is at the door. She misses nothing. Marie reports to her, I am sure of that.'

The boy heard his voice asking, 'Does she love him?'

'She has nothing else. It is a habit. She loves him in her way.'

It was strange – strange to be talking to his father, to discover secret lives. Yet it made a sort of sense.

'What happened between them?'

Don Raoul looked into his empty glass. 'When your mother left, there was a change. Besides,' he added, 'Alex cannot be said to have loved Thérèse. He loved your mother.'

Don Raoul had never mentioned her to the boy before. They were speaking in hushed voices, as if in the presence of the dead. Both were surprised at the ease with which they could speak. Curiosity had overcome the boy's sullenness, impending loss had weakened his father's reserve. The boy cradled the glass of sweet liquor and looked at him.

A shyness overcame Don Raoul: could the boy understand such adult matters? And then bitterness – still in the young face were his mother's features. Don Raoul looked away, into the dark, as if the window might show more than his reflection.

'Why did she go?'

'I do not know,' he said, stressing each word in a voice of anguish and rage. 'Fourteen years without her.'

He was reduced as with a fever, he could talk. But not about the important thing. How could the boy direct his father's attention to the subject that most concerned him – widen out the breach in the defences that had kept them strangers all his life?

'Has the doctor come?'

Don Raoul shook his head. 'It is too late for doctors. Besides, he wouldn't have one.' And then a dry laugh escaped him. 'He did call for a priest. I think you must have converted him. That little man from the village came. I'd not seen him for months. Alex sent word by Marie – he didn't ask me to have him fetched. I found him in his black cloak in the hall, trying all the wrong doors. Marie admitted him but failed to take him to your uncle's room. Such a long-nosed fellow, all crusted with dust from his walk here, puffing, whispering in his teeth as if praying: "Is this the room? Oh dear, a closet. Is it this?" He almost leapt out of his skin when I surprised him.'

71

The boy did not smile. 'Wouldn't a doctor have helped ease the pain?'

'Away with doctors!'

The spell between them was broken. 'Was I to drag a doctor here from Santa Marta to tell me what I know? My brother is dying.' Don Raoul covered his face with his hands. The boy watched him. His father would be alone entirely.

Don Raoul looked old when he uncovered his face. All in a moment, old. He tried to turn his thoughts from his apprehension of his brother. He had spent most of the afternoon beside him, until the harsh irregular breathing had eaten into his hearing. It sounded now, even when the sleeper was out of earshot. It would not cease to sound when the life was over. Looking on the ghostly, hunched figure of Tio Alex, he wondered if, by calling him to La Encantada, he had killed him long ago, that promising young man. 'Our Voltaire' his mother had called him. It was Paula who had engineered his exile, lured him there, and left him and her cousin, her husband and her baby – an enchantress who cast her spell and left her victims in it when she fled. He should have sent Alex back – and Thérèse, too. But he kept them – no, he let them stay, rather, not caring what happened.

Alex hugged the disease that had been sown in him when he was a child. He could hardly speak. Yet when he opened his eyes he saw, strong above him as always, his brother. He did not want to abandon Raoul.

When Raoul left him in painful slumber, stealthily Tia Thérèse occupied the straight chair by the bed. She too had become frail – a cage of bones, a shadow. Had Tio Alex come awake under her steady gaze, he would have said she was Azrael in a black gown. But he slept deeply and did not wake even when, after midnight, the boy came, kissed his forehead and went to the other bed in the familiar room.

'You can sleep elsewhere if you like,' his father said. 'You won't get much rest with his rasping.'

'This is my room.'

He heard all night, as his father had, the mechanical agony of his uncle's breathing. It crossed his mind that in all the days at San Mateo he had not prayed once for Tio Alex – or for anyone. He did not pray now, either, except to wish that Tio might answer his question, even if it wasted his last breath. His father suffered from apprehension of the end, but the boy knew nothing of death. While there was that terrible rasp of breathing, he could believe in miracles.

Next morning Tio seemed improved. He opened his eyes fully, wiped the phlegm from his own lips and raised himself a little on his pillow. He saw the boy was home, he smiled, gestured him to come near. The boy kissed his light, cold hand and sat down on the bed.

17

Tio Alex found his voice. 'I have been waiting for you. Your letters came.' Before the boy could speak, he went on in an urgent whisper. 'There is no secret. Pain has kept your father silent. This is the little I can tell you.' He subsided, gathered himself again.

During the boy's absence, he had emerged from delirium to the nightmare of the future – their future without him. There might be time to tell the missing story simply, to solve the tension between father and son. They were the only creatures that concerned him, divided by the same desertion. He started to speak, and as the day went on, painfully, sentence by sentence, he told the boy what he could.

Paula, he said, was strange – affectedly natural, vain yet unsure of her powers, immodest, in some ways shallow. He spoke of her with a hint of bitterness. The boy's face reddened to hear her spoken of at last. She began to exist.

Alex loved her almost as much as the boy's father did. Whatever she asked, he did. He remembered the fine hair on her skin, a few freckles that the voyage to La Encantada heightened, grey eyes never calm, except sometimes when she sat on the balcony and looked across the *campo* as though it did not exist, seeing France dancing before her in the haze.

Little wrinkles appeared around her eyes, not from smiling but from pain. They did not tell her age, but she was no longer twenty. He used to joke and say the moon had aged her hair. No, there was little repose about her. Her pulse showed in all her movements.

Because his uncle had loved her, the boy knew he would tell the truth.

After two years, she realized they had planned a mirage, not a future. France had seemed a desert: they were poor. They intended to climb out of poverty through her connections.

In marriages, a good family judges severely. In every sense, her choice of Raoul was a bad one. True, he had the graces to move among her class of people. But they were acquired graces. He had such habits because his parents had spoiled him. Alex was Voltaire, but he was the chosen one. In the south, people are too generous with their children.

Their father sold what he had – he was not poor – to keep Raoul a gentleman. Whatever he asked. Their deaths – they died within days of one another – were a disappointment. Raoul thought them richer than they were. They left a mortgaged estate and a blessing. The rest had gone on his clothes, carriage, the education that included gaming tables, drawing rooms, theatres.

He chose to marry Paula because she was engaged elsewhere. She was beautiful. He assumed she would bring a fortune with her. The man to whom she was originally betrothed was rich – old, perhaps, certainly unloveable. But worse matches have been made – she could have had Raoul as a lover. That was not good enough for him. She must be his. There was a scandal. She had to marry Raoul. Besides, she loved him.

He expected the dowry agreed for the other marriage. But her father gave only a reluctant blessing. Raoul continued to believe she would not be left destitute in his care. Alex warned him that it was possible. Raoul said a month would bring a settlement – if they lived poor on his doorstep, the old man would not bear the indignity. Alex had met her father and knew Raoul was wrong. His credulity proved that he had acquired no more than the colouring of her class.

Good families disown bad marriages. They cut off the offending branch. Raoul did not understand – the only parents he knew were his own, who beggared themselves for him.

He and Paula lived for several months with creditors on the stairs. They moved about, shedding debts. Even Alex who had nothing lent them money. They dined out among friends who watched them with fascination. In those months he actually fell in love with her. But she was changing. One evening he said he could live happily with her even as a pauper. She replied that she could not live happily as a pauper with anyone.

75

She sensed how fond he had grown, and she punished him, she made him jealous. Sometimes she refused to share his bed.

Their life was miserable, and so was Alex's. He was in love with her too. Not that he had hopes. But she had a way he could not explain.

At last her father came forward with a plan to put them at a distance. They were weakened by disappointment and so accepted. They went abroad to make their fortune quickly and return to do credit to their class. Her father gave them enough money to vanish entirely from his world.

Exile – it frightened Paula. But Raoul did not hesitate. He accepted the offer with both hands, hungrily. He thought he would have her to himself at last. Raoul went out first and she followed three months later – with Thérèse and Alex. By that time Alex had no choice in the matter.

For a year in their new life as *hacendados*, they were equally in love, clinging to the familiar things they shared. They lived for one another, hating the place. They had never worked before. He grew strong, riding in the fields, getting to know the land. When his wife and brother first arrived, they hardly recognized the swarthy rancher as the once urbane Raoul.

But she did not change except to become paler, more strange and wonderful. She made the house liveable. It had been stiff and formal – she somehow turned the angles into curves. When she finished making it her own, there was nothing more to do – no one to entertain, no one to woo her. Alex and Thérèse made her boredom more intense. And then she had a son, a squalling baby, and she loathed him.

They planned to prosper quickly and return. A bad summer destroyed their first hopes. Raoul said they should be patient. Paula said they would grow old.

The boy was conceived in their infatuation but born into their disappointment. He was a harbinger – more children, not one neighbour to call on. The Lebruns? They were provincials, Creoles. She found scorpions in the bedrooms, huge spiders in the drawing room, and rats. The servants were ignorant Indian girls, her child was sickly, the house by turns too hot to breathe in and then cold as a tomb.

Tio Alex shuddered, pulling the blankets closer round him though the room stifled the boy. The words that filled the void of his past were acid. He sat silent, waiting for his uncle to finish.

Raoul's love grew as hers lost direction among so many rooms. He spent whole days away in the far fields. She stayed among her books. They made her melancholy. The magazines came six months late and she read how her friends were growing into lives of consequence. She had been erased. When her child was born, her father sent a little christening mug, her favourite sister sent a coarse cotton petticoat. They seemed gifts of repudiation. The actual christening was celebrated in the chapel. It was the last time it was used. There were the four exiles, the baby and the priest. Her world was tiny.

Then she felt the pull of the blood – envy, anger and guilt. She turned against Raoul. Heine quotes the old play: 'She was adorable, and he adored her. But he was not adorable and she did not adore him.' She punished him. She neglected her child to punish him. Alex did not blame her. She was not to blame. It is how it was.

Tio Alex breathed shallowly and fast. He lay very still and his thin voice continued without expression.

She despised her baby's wailing, his damp face on her breast. He had her eyes, her features, but crumpled up. He reminded her by turns of each of her relations. She tried to provide for him. She chose Margarita whose yellow hair reminded her of home and who was intelligent. She could be trained. Though only twelve or thirteen at the time, she was made nurse. Paula waited until she was sure Margarita could be trusted. The girl made the baby stop crying. She sang and carried him up and down the courtyard.

There was love between the servant and her mistress. She treated her as a daughter. Even now Margarita sometimes had gestures taken from Paula.

Tio Alex told Paula to give herself up to her child. She was annoyed – as if to sacrifice her youth and beauty (she was no longer young) to such a calling was beneath her.

She sat sometimes at the spinet and played some old air. She played badly but with feeling. When Raoul came to listen, she closed the instrument and left the room. Still he loved her, burning the colder she grew.

There was no fortune to be made at La Encantada. Not quickly. Not while their place was – so to speak – still warm in

Paris. They found no repose; it was as though they never quite finished unpacking their bags, sure they would be departing soon. She chose to go, and went.

No one was to blame. And yet Alex realized that the boy must blame someone. He told him to consider it this way: his mother could not abide the present. She lived entirely on unreal hopes, and then on regrets for the wrong choices she had made. She needed to be admired, to be seen. Here she was invisible. She was afraid of time.

The boy moved to the window. He looked into the huge vacancy.

One day Raoul was at the far estate. She called the carriage, took one trunk with all her valuables and a few clothes, and set off for the railway halt. It was new then – Raoul had just had it built. The little platform was white and smelled of lime. Alex took her there himself. She said she was going for a week or two to the capital. She had gone before, impulsively like that. It was thought to be another brief adventure. After six weeks, they started to understand.

Alex could imagine her boat sailing from Veracruz, how she might have emerged on deck, light-headed. The green land steamed in the morning, then sank in the west. Returning, she thought she could unweave what had been done, recover lost years into her body, as though the boat sailed back through time, to Europe.

She sent a letter for Raoul in his brother's care a year after she left. Alex was to give it to him if he thought it right. But Alex read it and folded it again, placing it in one of her books. In Sévigné, the second volume. He never gave it to Raoul and he never answered her.

The boy had to lean close to catch the words. He raised his uncle's head to give him water. Then he listened for more, but his uncle's lips did not move. The boy cried out, 'Your blessing, Tio Alex!'

'If it is worth anything, God bless you.' He raised himself into a sitting position and, with an effort, his eyes brightened. 'Enough of the old story! Tell me where you have been.' But before the boy could speak, the eyes turned white. It happened in an instant, he was dead.

'Father!' the boy shouted. 'Father!'

78

18

Don Raoul was right. Tia Thérèse did not linger. She was found that afternoon at the window of her room, her face pressed against the pane, as when a child tries to see through its own reflection. She was looking towards El Abanico; early afternoon, blue piled high above the mountain.

19

By the time the undertaker arrived from Santa Marta, Marie had laid out the bodies. No one had instructed her to do so, but it was one of the duties she assumed – along with the altar lamp and other invisible charities. It was she who summoned Don Pepe.

He carried Doña Thérèse and Don Alejandro lightly, one over each shoulder, down the stairs. They were laid out in the dining room with its pinkish mahogany light and mirrors that repeated their pale profiles. Marie washed Doña Thérèse's face so that the lips were no longer crimson but grey and slightly parted. The good teeth shone like a row of pearls.

The undertaker was an old man who had buried several Obermullers. He was called Don Fidel.

'You will want it done properly,' he told Don Raoul.

'Of course,' the *patron* replied, too exhausted to ask further. 'I leave it in your hands.' He retreated to the lantern room.

Black crape was hung in abundant folds above the door. The boy, his father and the domestic servants were fitted out for mourning in more elaborate detail than during the festive arrangements for the Lebruns. Seamstresses came and a fat tailor from Santa Marta who rubbed his hands a good deal and used a wafer of chalk to mark the folds at sleeve and cuff. Each person was given instructions, so that on the day they would know their parts – parts that reflected their formal relations with the dead.

The peons wore solemn bands of crape on their right arms. The single bell in the village church tolled over the cane fields, and in reply, for the first time in years, the deep-toned bell of the hacienda chapel answered from its unfinished tower, shuddering through the house.

'If that bell is ever rung,' Tio Alex had said, 'the whole chapel will collapse in dust.'

Don Fidel the undertaker was soon in complete control. He even gave Don Pepe orders, and the terrified overseer ran to do his bidding. There was a demonic authority in the waspish little man with vast red and white sidewhiskers and crimson face and hands. He was old; he had seen more dead in his time than many generals do. He had exhausted two graveyards in Santa Marta and had opened a third on the road to San Mateo.

A team of peons gathered. The chapel door was thrown open and the undertaker led them in. In two days the nave was cleaned, the place restored as well as it could be. The mournful scent of lilies struggled against the reek of bats. The tomb lamps were relighted by the undertaker himself.

The boy remembered how the dining room and the east wing had been restored so suddenly, as if by magic, to accommodate the Lebruns: ceremony was restorative.

'You will not wish your family to share the Obermuller tomb,' Don Fidel told the *patron*. 'It would be improper and perhaps illegal.'

'Whatever you suggest,' said Don Raoul.

The undertaker's men set to work opposite that monument, excavating a tomb for the new family.

'Not too deep,' said Don Raoul. 'There are not many of us.'

'The carvings can come later,' said Don Fidel. 'You will want carvings, a family of your importance.'

'Later, yes.' Much later.

Don Fidel worked so briskly, with such a severe relishing of his task, that the whole house came alive. Marie and Margarita were favoured lieutenants, taking orders, bringing food, sheets, cotton. The old man took up residence in one of the better guest rooms. 'I am too old to travel all the way to Santa Marta, back and forth, each day. My nephew can look after the dead in town.'

He had not expected again in his lifetime to have a great funeral at La Encantada.

'You will, I assume, wish to bury both in the same vault,

despite the fact that they were only cousins by marriage.' Don Raoul nodded and turned away.

The undertaker's wagon brought two ornate coffins from the workshop in Santa Marta. They came through the high Dresden gate and were transported with difficulty into the house. They were tailored to different sizes. The one for Doña Thérèse was longer and shallower; for Don Alejandro, a shorter, deeper box was required to take his huddled form that, even in death, had not unclenched itself.

The boy stayed close to his uncle, helping to lift the empty body into its black and gilt container, clutching at the brass handle as if at a hand, and keeping vigil. Late into the night, alone with a candle and the body, he waited puzzled and unhappy. When, past midnight, his father came to join him, he left the room and went up to bed. Don Raoul was left to watch his brother.

On the morning of the funeral, the Dresden gate was opened and the courtyard filled with men and women from the fields. They stood with their black armbands just as they had done for the Obermuller funerals, waiting to see the corpses on their beds of silk and paper flowers and to receive largess. Sometimes they had come with actual grief, as if they had lost a parent, when a *patron* or his wife died and they knew a change would follow. They mourned genuinely when Don Carlos Obermuller died. In his son Otto they feared the changes that had come, and they were mourning for themselves.

Now they were only curious about two bodies. Was the woman not a witch, an *hechicera*? Some said she had driven off Doña Paula out of rage and jealousy, that the bad crops were caused by her spells. She appeared at the windows from time to time, a cloud, a pallor, and they crossed themselves and said an *Ave* as a precaution. A few remembered how Don Alejandro had ridden among them casually years ago, sometimes with the *patron*, later with the boy on his saddle. He had learned their names. They were sorry about him.

The open caskets were carried down into the courtyard by eight men brought specially from Santa Marta, all of them wearing formal liveries with the lugubrious self-importance of soldiers in dress uniform. The bells tolled once more. The dead were placed on trestles and the peons filed past and looked down on the departed. Don Raoul and his son stood on the steps and winced to see them passing. The women crossed themselves. The men raised their hands and touched the cheek or hand of Don Alejandro. 'For luck,' the undertaker whispered to Don Raoul. 'They take him for a hunchback.'

Tio Alex was displayed in a dark suit. He wore a green cravat fixed down with a gold pin. It looked as though a nail had been driven through him. His eye-whites showed in crescents, not quite sealed under the lids. It did not look like sleep. It looked like death.

Before the casket tops were fixed in place, the undertaker, dressed in sumptuous glowing black, led Don Raoul and the boy forward. 'Kiss them,' he hissed, and each in turn kissed the papery dead. Then the undertaker himself drew from out of one of his pockets the long brass screws, and the caskets were sealed down. The bearers stood to attention, hoisted the boxes on their shoulders, and went through the crowd to the gate. Outside, the little priest from the village waited with four acolytes, two with censers, two with holy water. The priest took the procession forward and it swayed left, down the north side to the chapel. The pace was the slow pace of the knell.

It fell to Don Pepe to scatter to the assembled peons the largess, the 'death money' as he scornfully called it, angry that the living labourers should be so rewarded. The cobbles were still strewn with straw. The crowd dispersed almost soundlessly, clutching their coins, murmuring in low voices.

Few mourners reached the chapel. Two were family. Marie was there, too, sitting without expression. Margarita had done her fair hair elaborately. It rose like a golden mitre above her dark face and gown. She had persuaded the undertaker, in return for her kindnesses, to order for her a particularly sumptuous gown: 'After all, I am the closest thing the boy has to a mother.' The bearers from Santa Marta whispered about her. She showed her grief to advantage, handkerchief in her fist, her eye wandering among the holy figures.

The little priest spoke. No music sounded but the bell kept throbbing. The caskets were lowered into the new vault, one above the other, and were covered. The boy remembered Isidro's question: how would they get out on Judgement Day? Perhaps they wouldn't try.

The bell stopped. Don Raoul and his son left the chapel, received condolences at the door, then walked briskly back to the house. There was no wake. Don Pepe was delegated to pay off the undertaker and his men. 'I am not to be disturbed by them again,' Don Raoul said.

He and his son vanished to their separate rooms. They had played their roles. They removed their stifling costumes.

20

After the preparations, the ceremony, the undertaker's exertions ('Very successful, I should say,' Don Fidel told Don Pepe when it was clear that he would not regain admittance to Don Raoul) the house was still, like a body resting after exercise. The two who died had hardly seemed presences, yet their absence was painful. For some days the boy and his father kept to their separate rooms. It was the boy's first experience of death. Also of a solitude to which there was no fixed term. His room grew large. He was lost in it with the books, yellow magazines, portraits that did not belong to him – inattentive, severe.

For Don Raoul the last root had been cut. Who was left to watch and respect him – to pity him? He had shared the indignity of exile with his brother. The flight of his wife had bonded them more closely. Alex was an extension of himself, a limb of memory. They had little need to speak. Through Alex he watched and loved his son with a remote jealousy. The loss of his brother seemed to entail the loss of the boy.

The courtyard was abandoned to the chickens. No one troubled to shoo them. Each afternoon Don Raoul watched. They seemed enormous as their shadows ran before them, behind them, busy at the dusty straw. They were gaunt, brown clouds of feather, strung together by a few bones. When Marie brought chicken for dinner, Don Raoul knew he would be hungry until the next meal. Yet they had been here since before he came, the chickens, like Marie and the peons. He could perceive no pattern in their motion – unless it was a panic of hunger as they tasted pebbles and the fallen oranges.

85

Then all at once they closed ranks. A girl came through the footgate. Her blonde hair was carefully braided and coiled above her dark face. She clucked and summoned the flock, smoothing her blue skirt and apron with both hands. She led them through the gate, clicking her tongue, and the yard was empty. Nothing moved at all, shadows gathered in a pool, welling upward. At evening a yellow mongrel came, nosed at the gate, and then squeezed through the bars. She sniffed the trunks of the orange trees, raised herself on hind legs to look into the weed-grown fountain. At first her presence annoyed Don Raoul. She came on Tuesday, then on Wednesday. He went to chase her away. But when he shouted at her she did not run. She sat down. He approached threateningly and she wagged her tail. He patted her.

Marie found scraps and Don Raoul christened his new companion Butter. She grew sleek and honey-coloured and slept by the door to his room or ran beside him when he walked out or rode. She guarded him.

The boy had no companion but he heard, day after day, his father's footsteps overhead. 'It must be money worries again – he's trying to walk away,' Tio Alex had said. This pacing had never been so regular and uninterrupted as now, late into the night, like a sullen mule turning a thresher round and round. 'It's a heartbeat,' the boy said. More than money worries made him walk. But when the girl came for the chickens in the courtyard, the footsteps paused. When she led her brood out through the footgate, they resumed. Had he been walking a straight line, he would have covered the distance to Veracruz, or even as far as that done by the Crusaders who went from Paris to Jerusalem.

The big heat came – not bright but dull, the dust suspended in the air like smoke. The boy drew the curtains across the windows. Moths had been busy and had made small sequin-holes of light. A dappled twilight shone. The English barometer was stuck at FAIR. He tapped it with his finger but the needle insisted. He lay on the dead man's bed. The weight of his father's worry held him there, unable to doze or read. He lay stunned with the heat and with his uncle's absence. Late in the afternoon he parted the curtains, opened the door and stepped on to the balcony. The hanging plants and pot plants, long unattended, trailed stems and crisp leaves across the view. The grape arbour was brittle, its fruit the bundles spiders made out of their prey. The railway line wound out of the haze. Gradually the falling sun coloured the air: pink stipples spread and merged. At last the sky was one towering redness, like the heart of a coal. Then it cooled.

21

Three weeks after the funeral, Don Raoul sent Margarita for his son. The boy crawled off the bed and climbed the stairs as he was, pale and rumpled. When he knocked at his father's door, the dog yapped.

'Good afternoon,' his father said, in a tone that tried to be genial. The dog made noises in its throat.

The boy stood very still. His father took him by the shoulders and drew him towards the light.

'Are you ill, too? Your skin has gone just like Alex's.'

'It is the heat.'

His father looked doubtful, pointed to a chair. The boy sat down. After a pause, Don Raoul began.

'It is time we began to share La Encantada.' He unfolded his plan with something like enthusiasm. The boy would study the ledger books, map and records. He would ride out with Don Pepe and get to know each acre and each peon. 'I used to know them all by name.' They would come to recognize him as another *patron*.

The boy stared at his palms. His father had prepared a speech, rehearsing it as he made that ceaseless thunder that kept his son suspended, as if waiting for a storm. It was a plan to bind him to the place, to close the gate of the cage. He, too, was to be a sacrifice to the estates. *Patron* indeed! But he heard, glancing at his father's face from time to time. How unfamiliar he was, how unused to persuasion. He did not invite the boy's comment or assent by tone or gesture. He was simply declaring his will, as though it were quite natural that, after so many neglected years, a father should lay claim to his son. The years were in Don Raoul's face, long lines cut deep about the mouth, and in his voice, which though firm had grown remote and tired. He spoke from the tunnel of his thoughts.

The speech was long. The squat gold-faced clock chimed the quarter, the half hour. The boy had never heard his father use so much language. He was like a man talking in his sleep. His son sat still for fear he might waken him or prompt a direct question. The boy knew himself vulnerable to his father. He had nowhere to go.

At last Don Raoul ran out of words. He settled into his chair. His eyes indicated that it was now time for the boy to speak. But the boy said nothing. He stared at his hands as if he had heard nothing. The silence lasted some minutes. Don Raoul had offered all he had and waited for a reply. For gratitude. Surely so great a manifest of trust would shift the boulder of estrangement.

He prompted him at last. 'Well, what do you say?'

'It is so much . . . I am too tired to think just now.'

'You do not need to think! It is quite natural. We have no choice – we cannot leave here, either of us.'

'Never?'

His father would not abandon the old illusion so completely. 'We have no means to do so at this time.'

'We could sell up! Tio Alex always said we could sell up one day, the way the last Obermuller did!'

'Not now, not with the troubles. Who would buy, when already to the north . . .' He stopped himself. 'There are always rumours of trouble to the north.' And yet along the coast, too – some weeks the train could not run at all, and when it came, it carried soldiers and supplies. On the coal car and the guard's van, guns were fixed. He had a letter from the state government requiring him to supply soldiers for the Santa Marta garrison.

'We cannot sell. In fact, even if the troubles are all rumour, no one would buy La Encantada now. The yield is too low.'

'Tio Alex told me about El Abanico. He said our real wealth lay at our backs, in the mountain. He took me to the mine.'

Don Raoul snorted. 'Alex and his fantasies!' Then, more gently: 'We all have our fantasies here. You will find new ones no doubt. My fantasy is irrigation: if I could get water to the big fields towards Santa Marta, we would transform La Encantada.'

'Is the mountain not rich?'

'Only to the rich who can afford to make it so. To open up El Abanico – what would it cost? And do you think the Obermullers would have let the mine die if there were still money in it?'

'Perhaps the peons did not wish to dig it any longer.'

'Men do what they are paid for.'

Don Raoul took his son's questions as acquiescence in the plan. 'Come at noon tomorrow. We will work out a schedule – two days a week with Don Pepe, the rest here with me and the records, and sometimes a trip to Santa Marta, or even to the capital for provisions.' The boy thought of Don Pepe, with whom he had hardly exchanged a word in his life, whom he despised because Isidro had despised him. He thought of the records – tomes that now recorded loss, the pace of loss. He kept these reflections to himself.

He left silently. The dog growled, but kept its head on its paws.

At noon the next day, he locked the door of his room. At one o'clock, Margarita knocked.

'Your father is calling you!'

He did not answer her. He lay on the shadowy bed, thinking of Tio Alex with the other corpse. And of his mother. And of France. Of the heat.

At two, his father knocked. Still he did not answer. His father hammered on the door with a closed fist. After a pause he heard Don Pepe's shrill note: 'We must break the door.' A splintering as the overseer hurled himself into the room. He dusted his shoulder and looked round as if expecting to see another death. Behind him, drawn with expectation, Don Raoul; and framed in the door, Margarita and Marie.

They looked for the boy in the dimness. Then Don Raoul whipped back the curtains. White light fell upon his brother's bed where the boy lay quite still, his eyes open. The four came forward. Don Raoul took the wrist between the fingers.

'Still warm. The heart is beating.'

At that moment the boy screamed: 'Close the curtains! The light is hurting me!'

His father was convulsed with rage.

'She left when you were two, and here you lie, just like her! Let the damned light burn him!' he shouted at Marie who had hurried to draw the curtains together. 'Let him burn! Damn the woman, damn her child!'

He led the way. The servants followed him. Don Pepe slammed the door once, twice, but the lock was broken. It drifted ajar. Marie came later with a wire and fixed the catch.

In the months that followed, only Marie came, tending him like a nurse. He lay quite still, sitting up to eat what she brought him and to be washed. He grew so weak that it was an ordeal to stand beside the bed while she changed it. She did not speak and he, too, remained silent. He was not grateful to her, for if she had not come he might have died.

22

In the boy, Don Raoul had found his wife again, this time unable to flee. And he would punish her. He would close her out entirely. 'The light hurts!' the boy had cried, as if with Paula's voice, out of a pain to which Don Raoul had no access. He was being blamed, yet he had offered all he had to give – La Encantada itself.

Still, he fretted. It was not guilt – rather, disappointment of the desire to have his son beside him. Alex's wish had been that they should come together. It was the aim of his long, loving education. So Don Raoul waited, as he had for years after Paula's departure, for a return, a footstep on the stair, an apology that need not even be in words – a simple gesture would suffice, an acknowledgement. The boy did not come.

Margarita came each day to clean the lantern room. She brought him meals on a flowered enamel tray. She even tried to talk with him. She was no longer the little nursemaid who always sang and carried the baby in her shawl. He liked it when she was in his room. She reminded him of Paula, and of the boy when he was still small and would let himself be set upon the table where the ledgers were and spoken to in the silly, cheerful way parents use. Margarita had learned something from her mistress. There was about her movements, as if in caricature, the abrupt grace of his wife, the sudden flashes of expression which, whatever she was saying, betrayed her feeling. She was now almost as tall as his wife, and though her darker skin and Indian features entirely lacked the delicacy of the model, memory grew dull and, in her, the hints of an earlier life came into focus. She was young.

Whatever she did was addressed to him. Even when she wandered in the courtyard, gathering the chickens, she was not walking, quite: she seemed to dance.

One day he rummaged in an old trunk and found some of Paula's dresses. He chose one he remembered. The creases had yellowed, but the girl cleaned it and wore it for him. It seemed to suit her. It was almost a new pleasure to give delight to someone in this way, and he indulged it, giving her scarves, hats, shoes, raiding the trunks of clothing he had never thought to open again in his life. Garment by garment she assumed the remaining wardrobe of her mistress.

It did not occur to him that he was foolish, that the world continued beyond the confines of the lantern room and the other servants might think ill of it. He concentrated upon her. Don Pepe saw which way the wind was blowing and encouraged him. He said the servants were talking ill of her and that she should be set apart from them. After five weeks, Don Raoul approached her.

'You should not be living with the servants.' He gave her three rooms in the east wing, as far from the servants' quarters as possible. Now she too was alone. And he went to her there.

It was his first infidelity and in it – more than pleasure – was relief, and an additional revenge. Had it not been for Alex, he might have singled her out earlier. But the presence of his conscience, as he now regarded his brother, and of his son restrained him. Now both were dead. He savoured his freedom with the girl.

It broke the last sentimental ties with the past. He no longer dreamed of France. He had started again, in the place where he thought himself damned. She drew him down from the lantern room into a kind of intimacy. She gathered in her apartment things from all over the house – the engravings of Maximilian and Carlotta, candlesticks, little boxes, cushions, porringers. She made a boudoir, partly at his instruction; and she learned an eager and increasingly subtle sensuality with him. He came to depend upon her – upon the knowledge that she waited for him in her jumbled room. He did not criticize her or the things she gathered around herself. After all, when he was not with her she could not go back among the servants. She was condemned to wandering the rooms of the old house. She might as well take

93

what she wanted. She saw her advantage growing. Three months after Don Alex was buried, she was pregnant by the *patron* of La Encantada.

Don Raoul was fascinated by her hair. In her, he found a fragment of his race in exile, but transformed, revived. 'We may be cousins,' he said. She let him brush her hair or watch her braid it tight with red and black ribbons.

Occasionally he saw the swarthiness of her face, the high cheekbones; the Indian was dilated, the French effaced. He would sicken with disgust and stay away from her for a day or two. But not for long. The solitude of the lantern room became unbearable at night.

By degrees she grew harder, more assured, the candid eyes of the nursemaid changing with the anxiousness of calculation.

'If I knew that Paula was dead, I would marry you,' said Don Raoul, safe in the belief that he would never know. It was that security she craved: to be recognized. The loss of her mistress had damaged her almost as much as it had her lover. She worshipped Doña Paula as young men worship heroes. When the boy was a child and asked about his mother, she would say, 'She has gone on a journey, but she will be back. No mother could desert her child for ever.' She was as much Paula's child as the boy was. Now she feared her mistress might return. She prayed that she might be dead and news reach them.

The reflections of his wife that Don Raoul originally perceived in Margarita had been accidental, echoes. Now she began to imitate her memory of the French woman, doing her hair in her style, talking a little like her, acting now sullen and now friendly. If only she could be sure of him! But she could not be sure of anything.

What future would she have as a servant here if Don Raoul tired of her? The other servants resented and blamed her. She had few friends outside the hacienda – she had let her rest days pass casually, within the walls, without advantage. She had never gone back to her *pueblo*. A sister or a cousin might call, but La Encantada was her home; she had no other.

She became mistress to retain it and the life to which her parents had deserted her. They had sold her when she was a child. Doña Paula took her for a servant because of her pretty hair. She paid them well.

She could not read, but she could see, and she wasted no impression. Now she planned each step she took. Don Raoul was alone; his eyes gave everything away.

She took to standing at the Dresden gate in her fine gowns, proclaiming herself the lady of the place. At first, an old peon or a woman from the village would greet her in passing.

'Margarita! God be with you. How well you look.'

She rejected the greeting. She taught them that she was no longer one of them. If she braided her hair as the Indians do, she then coiled it on the crown of her head, the way Paula did, a snake of gold.

Then she asked for her own servant, because as a lady and, soon, a mother, she would need assistance and the servants who already tended Don Raoul would not come near her. She chose a girl from Santa Marta, not from the village.

Later, when Margarita was nursing, Don Raoul saw the bruise-coloured nipples long and smooth, like the sharp heads of birds.

The servants changed. Margarita communicated her distrust to Don Raoul, and they were dismissed one by one to return to the fields or to find work elsewhere. Only Marie stayed on – she was so quiet, almost part of the air that moved slowly through the corridors, a pair of hands and eyes, but never speaking.

The others Margarita replaced at her whim, and frequently. Half-forgotten relations were introduced in the old livery. They could neither clean nor cook. Don Raoul was growing passive, coarse. He overlooked the changes.

He came to La Encantada out of the refinement of love. The second love took off his brilliance. The land that belonged to him by deed was slipping away. He protected himself from the loss by easing roots into the dry soil resignedly, calling Margarita 'wife' as she neared her time, but unable to make her one. He was becoming worse than a Creole, a mestizo, devising a future with his body, a future that even a year before he would not have believed desirable.

He was almost glad that Alex was gone. There were no witnesses.

She wore a gold medallion of the Virgin of Guadalupe at her neck. But she no longer attended church in the village: the eyes that watched her were curious, and she could hear them whispering when she carried her pregnancy outside the Dresden gate.

She missed going to church. She had been devout in her way. She had taught the boy his prayers long before Don Alejandro filled his mind first with scepticism, then with theology. They had prayed at night and in the morning, they had said the rosary. They had even kept Doña Paula's icons for a time and lighted candles by the bed, until Don Alejandro had laughed them out of it in his gentle way: 'Idolaters!'

Her sin became public. It set her above the people she hired and then dismissed from service. They said that she had seduced him. She had dishonoured her family (though her family profited). She stole from Don Raoul to buy their approval – she stole money, little trinkets, provisions. If he noticed, he said nothing. His desire had made her indispensable. It had also made her a solitary. Like Doña Paula, she was an exile, but in the very place where she was born.

Don Raoul might have preferred a quiet mistress, but Margarita was not quiet. Once, in an excess of self-importance, she had the carriage brought round to the Dresden gate. In her borrowed gown, carrying a bright parasol, she crossed the courtyard and was handed into the carriage by a coachman whose threadbare livery went back to the time of the Obermullers. The carriage swallowed up the woman and her maid. The dusty panes drained their faces of colour. They became grey like the carriage itself, which had been woken from a long dream. It lurched to Santa Marta and the dust rose in puffs and billows with each pothole.

In Santa Marta she entered the main store to make purchases. She returned angrily the stares of those who dared to eye her, unless they were people she took to be important. The manager in charge of the Lebrun estates near Santa Marta – he was known as 'the viceroy' – approached in the street. She placed herself where he could not avoid her. So he doffed his hat and asked, 'How is the *patron*?' She did not forgive him that.

When she called on the priest at the parish church, he received her stiffly in the cloisters. Gossip was not confined to La Encantada. The worst outrage was that she visited Our

Lady of the Plain, lighted a candle there and knelt for half an hour praying.

She crossed the plaza between the kiosk and the squat palm trees, moving like a rare bird with a huge head-dress. For her pregnancy she chose just the gowns that accentuated her condition. A stranger might have thought her an eccentric personage, but those who sat about the square or astride their horses outside the *cantina*, their faces concealed by the shadows of their hats, knew she was only Margarita, Santoya's youngest daughter, a servant and a whore – clever to be sure, but still a whore. How could she feel safe when those familiar, disrespectful eyes regarded her? 'I've done better than the lot of them,' she told herself, and sailed across the open space in full sunlight. She was safe because she carried Don Raoul's child.

Along the road that led from Santa Marta to La Encantada, the peons stopped working to watch the passing carriage. They did not acknowledge her, as they would have done had she passed on foot, a servant, one of them. Pushing their hats back on their heads, they watched the lurching vehicle and the grey lady and her maid behind its windows.

They used to salute the carriage, or Don Raoul when he passed on horseback. If he spoke to them, they remembered every word he said and related it in the village. Now he had changed – he never looked them in the eye or spoke cheerfully, he had forgotten their little problems, even their names. It happened all in a few months. He hardly rode out after the funeral. He had taken in the ill-omened yellow mongrel that had haunted the village for weeks till they drove it off. Now everywhere he went, it followed him, snapping and barking at those from whom it had begged. If the peons saw Don Raoul coming now, they turned aside, intent on their labour. They replied sullenly. The climate had changed.

When Doña Paula left, they understood. The pull of her world or the harshness of theirs defeated her. He stayed on and they were grateful for this, their solitary *patron*, judge of their disputes, physician of their illnesses. He had been more generous than the Obermullers – too generous maybe. The peons prospered less, but loved him. He paid for the treatment of the sick, even for visits from the doctor from Santa Marta. He paid for the burial of children and the old. He failed to insist on certain dues of rent and labour. Their bondage was relaxed.

Now that had altered and it was the woman's doing. Why had he chosen her, common woman, some said loose even before she worked on him and possessed him?

She interposed herself between him and his men.

'They are my people,' she said. 'I understand them better than you do. Things have gone badly because you have been lazy with them.'

Old regulations were imposed once more, though they yielded little profit.

'We are not rich – we must do what is just.' She taught him to think her harshness wise. He became less liberal.

If a peon came with a petition, Margarita intercepted him.

'My business is with the *patron*.'

'Don Raoul is engaged,' she said, with unnatural correctness. She no longer wore an apron. Her hands, which were now smooth, rested on her hips. She looked like a bright amphora with two almost graceful handles. One day she was roses, the next day terracotta. The top was always dark face and bright hair.

'It is urgent, Margarita.'

She disliked such familiarity.

'His own work is urgent, too. He is with Don Pepe.'

'My son is sick.'

'His own son is very sick.' The illness of the peon's child did not touch her – she was carrying the child of Don Raoul.

'I want two days off work and something for the burial.'

'Is he dead?'

'Today, tomorrow.'

'I will speak to Don Raoul. As for money, I can tell you there is none.' Then, rotating on the pointed shoes that pinched her feet and put her in ill-humour, she left the peon at the Dresden gate and went indoors. She did not trouble her lover with the request.

Once she was well established, the peons learned to pay court to her.

'Doña Margarita,' they said deferentially, 'I do not wish to trouble the *patron*. Can you help me?'

'What is it, Perez?' She used the surname, as Don Raoul did.

'My wife is ill. I need the doctor from Santa Marta. She is expecting and has too much pain.'

'Poor woman. I will speak to Don Raoul.' As intercessor she prevailed, brought a little money and permission to borrow a horse from the stable. The peon would repay her a portion of the money, her commission, and leave with a 'God bless you.'

'You were once poor, you understand us.' And she did understand them.

Don Raoul seldom knew who had come to his gate. He lent a trusting ear to her. She turned him against her enemies. If someone showed her disrespect, or was heard saying things against her, Don Pepe was sent. There was no longer any need to send offenders to El Manantial. A worse exile was offered by the garrison, and still Don Raoul had not supplied his quota.

Margarita's best weapon was her lover's jealousy.

'Beto was saying things,' she reported. That meant 'paying court'.

'To you? Beto the canalman was saying things to you?'

Whether true or false, the accusation worked. Beto, or some other peon, found himself summarily sent to Santa Marta, wearing an uncomfortable uniform and marching up and down with a stick on his shoulder.

She was the lens through which he saw his peons. He had estranged her from her people; she in turn deprived him of their love. All that she said, he took to heart. Only his son who lay as if lifeless in the room below his own escaped her calculations. And Don Pepe.

23

Don Pepe was growing fat. He had two gold teeth and a fine new hat with silver braid around the black crown and brim. Adjusting to the change in circumstances, he stood patiently in the courtyard every morning, waiting to be summoned. He prodded his spurs thoughtfully with a riding crop, shaking his head back and forth to keep the flies away, as if answering 'no, no, no' to a question. 'No, no, no' and then he slapped his cheek.

He edged into the shade of the blind arcade, leaned against the wall and let his eyes range over the high façade, casually appraising it, not letting the gaze rest on detail. Sun sparked the gold of his teeth. He had climbed a long way to arrive so nearly at the threshold of La Encantada. Everything was possible, as he told Don Raoul, everything is possible if you have time and money.

When he was summoned, his eyes dulled with a rehearsed servility. Holding his hat to his chest, he climbed the stairs.

He used another face in the fields – bared teeth for the peons, out of whose ranks Don Raoul had raised him. Now Margarita goaded him, subdued him. He had encouraged Don Raoul to pursue her. He had seen the lie of the land before the rest. Briefly he had been his master's confidant, and Margarita was in his debt.

Margarita had been dazzled by him ever since she was a girl. The boy used to tease her when he caught her eye following him across the courtyard. 'He'll be your husband one day, you'll see.' Now Don Pepe admired her.

She waited for him on the first landing to show him up to the lantern room: His step was slow now, ringing on the stairs. He breathed heavily and stood steaming on the landing. 'Ah, the young *patron*,' he said outside the boy's room, as much to pause and catch his breath as out of real concern. 'How is he?'

She shrugged.

'He should have a new horse. His old mare is fit for glue and nothing else. Eight months without a regular rider is too long.' Lugubriously he added, 'It seems years since I last saw him. I was young then, eh, Margarita?'

'Were you, Don Pepe? Back then, were you young?'

His shrill voice had drawn labour from the peons, maize and sugar cane from the fields. Straw and adobe houses, fields of cane so big they would have sweetened cities had the rains come on time. Don Pepe enjoyed power. 'So thin a voice in a man as stout as that,' Tio Alex said, 'a flute rising from a trombone. There's a hungry man under that corpulence.'

When Don Pepe was admitted to the *patron*'s presence, Margarita withdrew. But she could not resist; she slipped silently back up the stairs and set her ear against the wood. The men paced for a time, and then Don Pepe's footsteps ceased. Voices came as tones, not words, through the wood.

Don Raoul could seldom engage the dog-eyes of Don Pepe Ayala. The overseer understood him, however, sympathized with his agitation in tones reassuring, deferential.

After half an hour, Margarita precipitated herself down the stairs as quietly as she could. Don Raoul opened the door and released Don Pepe who came slowly down, with something of the air of a priest troubled by a too-frank confession. He called a loud farewell to Don Raoul. Then he addressed the mistress of the house.

'How is the little one?' He tapped her midriff with a fat forefinger. 'When does he come?'

'Why do you say *he*?'

'Ah, Doña Margarita.' He winked. 'Out of this' – glancing around at the high hallway, and with the look suggesting the whole estate – 'out of this, you would not expect a daughter!'

Their conversation was a play of tones and hints, a private, disclosing language. She asked for news.

'Things could be better. But they could be worse. There is nothing to fear. Troubles, yes, troubles, but still far off . . . Nothing to fear, yet.' He tried to rouse her anxiety and allay it.

'Don't worry – there are good horses in the stable still, and I have a good horse too.'

'And the fire at El Manantial?'

'It was no accident.'

'Damage?'

'The place is gone, every roof, every stick.'

'Where have the people gone?'

'They have become air.' He paused. 'They have gone into the hills.'

'What will they do?'

'Starve for a while. And then, in time, come down to us.' It pleased him to see her shudder.

'And the horses, Don Pepe – who stole the horses at La Serenita?'

'Thieves!' he exclaimed with a burst of mirth. 'Goodbye, Doña Margarita.' He kissed her hand and stepped into the sunlight, took a large breath, shrugged his round shoulders.

From his black horse he glanced upward to the lantern room, touched his wide hat to the *patron* who watched, and to the woman standing in the doorway. He rode slowly, in the direction of Santa Marta. The dusty road rolled up behind him.

24

The boy began to rouse from his torpor. He had no memory of the months lost lying on his back. Still he lay there, but his ears and eyes began to work. He heard the train. The sound of hoofs. He grew fretful, trying to find himself in the big room. There were figures there, looking down out of the shadows from large frames. Strangers.

A painter had done them all in 1881. He came from Europe and toured the provinces, going from estate to estate with his easel. He came to La Encantada after two months with the Lebruns. Here he invented the whole Obermuller family by his art. He invented faces for the dead. Heinrich was a severe, Rembrandtian, rust-coloured man. Following the family's evolution, the artist showed a relaxation, each generation younger than the last, more prosperous and serene. Otto, the youngest, in his teens, wore a Prussian uniform, his pink hands on the hilt of a sword.

Before his illness, the boy had been grateful for the company the pictures gave. He liked the backgrounds. Old Heinrich was flanked by the Dresden gate, emblem of his destiny. His son stood on the steps of the house, hardly altered in essential features. Heinrich's grandson stood stiffly at a window and behind him El Abanico was rendered almost alpine, with a lacing of gold and sunlight. Otto stood before a prospect of Dresden, as though the picture had been painted there.

Now the figures were not company. They seemed to rise from the Obermuller tomb and perch around his bed. They had created the place in which he lay, its suffocating calm.

Otto hung above the fireplace over a mantel-shelf of Italian marble diamonded with native onyx. Sometimes in winter Tio Alex lighted fires in the hearth and drew up chairs. They watched the heat together. Through flames, the little Dutch backing-tiles with their scenes of distant cities – Prague, Vienna, Munich – blue on white, as though drawn with a sky pencil on snow, remained cool, unpeopled, a glazed spire, a haze of trees.

The boy had chosen nothing in the room.

The books were his mother's for the most part, with here her maiden name, here her married name on the plates, so he could tell which reading shaped her expectations and which comforted her disillusion. Before she married, she read chiefly novels, but later, poetry. She marked the margins not with comments but with stars, her big and little sighs and approbations. How well the poets read her *ennui*, refining her desires. She read uncritically, looking for what she wanted to see. In a book of ballads, he counted seventy pencilled stars. He read each line she marked in order to deduce her from it.

Now she was remote, with everything else. As for him –

Ah! les petits mort-nés
Ne se dorlotent guère!

25

His torpor was not natural. The clock picked its way among the hours – Marie wound it once a week. Breakfast arrived. He ate. The tray was removed. He gazed around the room. Lunch came, he ate, the tray was removed. He slept or, with eyes closed, followed a thought, or saw some object as if for the first time – a vase, the swords above the writing table, the pistols that hung over the wash-stand, the blue and white porringer with its memory of scent. Tea came, he sipped it. The slightly parted curtains drew his eye. He measured the shadows. Supper, the same. Marie put out the lamp. Far off, a bell sounded, the train hooted on its way to the coast . . .

The women who had lived here spent listless days, hemmed into a solitude so constrained that, by noon, to breathe at all was an act of will.

He heard Margarita's voice grown loud and harsh. She did not come in – he heard her on the stairs. His father's pacing continued without destination. Occasionally a dog close by released a torrent of barking. The boy had fallen asleep in his uncle's bed and come awake in an altered world.

He began to sense his body, grown fat and weak. There was no way of finding out how long he had been ill. Marie did not say. She tended him faithfully: for her, he had taken the place of Tia Thérèse.

He was slow to wake completely to who he was. Tio Alex was dead, of that he was sure. Marie gave him cool sweet medicine distilled from leaves. Twice a day she fed it to him. Now he actually tasted it, sugar drowning a bitter, earthy flavour. Though she washed and combed him, changed the bed, kept his life from guttering, he felt that even she had become strange.

He dreamed they had hung crape at the windows. Marie spoke to the air, but he could hear her. 'There's a funeral wreath on the door.' Footsteps sounded in the courtyard, a crowd. Someone was dead. For a terrible hour, he thought it was his father. (Why else had he ceased to come?) They closed the curtains so it would be known that grief was in the house.

No one had died. He woke and felt a tingling in his remote limbs. He counted the joints as they came back, welcoming his body piece by piece.

One day he crawled from his bed, wrapped a sheet around his shoulders and staggered to a chair beside the hearth. When Marie entered, she found the bed empty. Then he moved his hand and, in a voice rusty with disuse, croaked out, 'I am here, Marie.' She turned and saw him seated in the chair, wrapped in a sheet, a book on his knee. She clapped her hand to her mouth.

'I am not a ghost, Marie,' he said. She resumed her work. His eyes rested on the page before him. It was a volume of the letters of Madame de Sévigné.

26

His mother's letter had been slipped into the second volume. Dust must have lain deep on those volumes even when his mother had lived here. So neglected was this collection of Sévigné letters that the pages had only been cut here and there, haphazardly. It was 27 May 1675. The frail pages of his mother's letter floated into his lap. He gathered them up, four closely written sheets, sent from Dijon and dated in the third year of his life.

Distance was prison, her husband's attentions circumscribed her until she found it difficult to catch her breath, etc. And yet now . . .

'When we arrived,' she wrote, 'the boy you bought the place from simply left. He climbed into a carriage and departed. The gate closed on us and we stayed like birds, my dear, wings clipped by poverty, gazing through the bars . . .' It was pretty. He glanced at the page of Sévigné, as if spanning in an instant more than two centuries to her cool, durable love, setting it beside the rapid, garrulous confusion of his mother's letter. 'My dear', 'my love', little puffs of sentiment to blow up the coal of her affection, punctuated her letter.

Madame de Sévigné had a more precise heart: '*Quel jour, ma fille, que celui qui ouvre l'absence!*' The words did not fade.

The boy wept for the old woman's love: if he had been born a daughter, a little Madame de Grignan, he would not have been abandoned. He felt cold, sitting in the deep chair, swaddled in a sheet and in his hand her book, her letter. 'I think of you, my dearest, I think of you all the time and long for you in the night. All here is familiar but incomplete without you.'

But Doña Paula was a slave of memories, a past more public and assured, where she was admired and courted. 'I loved you, I love you, but *here*, my darling, not in the wastes of La Encantada.' She would not squander her beauty on alien air. Her mirror instructed her: there were the expressions she had ceased to use in exile – they were intact. All they needed was society. Her flight was a drama she devised, but in secret, with no curtain to deliver her back to the world.

> *Je me livrerais, verte encore,*
> *De la branche me détachant,*
> *Au zéphyr qui souffle à l'aurore,*
> *Au ruisseau qui vient du couchant.*

'My dear, it was impossible, the place, the hateful rooms.' The word *free* signalled youth, family, property – early restraints so subtly applied that they seemed natural and enabling. If she discovered that the freedom she bought was in fact a movement in untrammelled space, in a perpetual present, without love, he did not know. 'How is the child?' She did not write his name! How young she must have felt when the boat slid from the quay at Veracruz and she was going home to an imagined welcome, the knot of her wilfulness unravelled by what she considered a renunciation.

Je me livrerais. Lines at the corners of her eyes, stretchmarks below her breasts and on her sides from childbearing, faded. The gold timepiece she carried ran backwards as she watched the ship's wake widen to the west. Land emerged out of the east like a bank of fog and there she vanished.

27

Several nights he climbed out of bed, went to the chair and took up the same book. Only one passing reference to himself in the letter – 'and the child?' After a year he had shrunk to that, a reflex of consciousness.

Yet she held him in a snare. She was *in* him. Don Raoul saw her in him. The boy's hand rested on the paper her fingers had moved over in a burst of qualified desire. He was filled with anger.

It was not easy to blame her for her flight – a social woman in a loneliness intensified by a husband's trusting inattention, in a house built by others who had filled it with their distinctive, sober contentment. The place was full of echoes that she could not interpret. She had foreseen the years it promised, the dust falling and falling, wiped away until the hand failed and disappointment buried what once seemed possible. Yet it was still just possible. 'We are young, Raoul, there is time, even if we are poor.' She had come round too late. 'In France, in the provinces, among orchards and vineyards, a humble place . . .' Was she so changed? '. . . Even if we are poor.' The boy did not believe her. If what she wrote were true, Tio Alex would have known. He would have handed the letter to Don Raoul and urged him to go home.

It was Don Raoul who had prised Paula free from a safe match, welcomed exile and shaped the dream of independent wealth. He taught his wife by example how a child may treat its parents, how a parent's devotion maims a child. Dragging her from what she knew, wanting her entirely to himself, he wooed her with projects – the French garden, for instance, planted with trees for shade, blossoms to please her. 'It will grow if you tend it,' he had said, to draw her out of doors and to interest her in the seasons. But sun cracked the soil. All that survived was a rose tree that each year exploded in small, indignant flowers.

Don Raoul worked because he loved her, and that became an affront.

'I am having the joiner make a boat. We can go rowing on the main canal.'

'It is really far too hot, Raoul.'

'He is making it with a canopy, like the boats at Xochimilco.'

'We will look ridiculous to the peons.'

Another time he announced: 'We will have the Lebruns come and stay.'

'They are not welcome.'

'They are our neighbours.'

'The Lebruns! Creoles! Do you imagine they still speak French after all those generations here? Do you imagine we could so much as *talk* to them?'

Don Raoul's charm was effaced in labouring to turn their exile to account. The polish of his manners that had drawn her in the first place was dulled by actual love, and then by labour. She saw him make the peons work to extract what could be got from the soil, all to be offered up at the altar of herself. Meanwhile she waited weeks, months, a year, fretful, dozing, sewing, reading in her room.

'Your child is your vocation.'

'And what are servants for?'

In those solitudes, she thought, 'We may return to France one day, but with no fortune, and old.' She woke from their dream to the vista of empty fields, hideous mountains.

'Have you resolved to stay on here for ever?'

'Not for ever, a little longer.'

'Time passes very fast for a woman.'

'Those lines aren't age. You frown too much.'

'They are lines of pain, Raoul. The baby cries and cries, there is no talking to him. You want more children? I would unmake that child if I could.'

So she woke from the dream and made another dream.

The boy too had a dream of Europe, though he would never go there. Like the Lebruns, he was a Creole and belonged precisely nowhere. If his father had not interfered, Paula might have married the dull rich man and the boy now have been beside the Rhône at a large estate with friends and horses, hunting; or in Paris at the *lycée*. His dream excluded his father. It was invention – yet the imagined ways we miss our lives are sometimes the best part of life. He was born between worlds and belonged to neither, though he imagined both. He was a bird that drifted over groves and forests where others settled. Even his father, with the servant girl.

28

Once he had known the peons. There was Isidro. More remotely he remembered the other boys – Paco, Juan, Jesus – all men now, he could see them from the window. With long bright machetes they went about the fields. Had they retained any of the candour they had as children? Or did nothing in their brief childhood detain them, no happiness, no loss? Perhaps they shed childhood as a snake sheds skin, or passed it – some of them – into new children. If only he could be like them – *be* one of them, poor, strong, uncomplicated. Watching them, he felt how unformed he had remained, a dune rolling before moving air, not to break but to become and become.

When he remembered their houses – he had visited Isidro against his father's orders – it was clay and grass he smelled, yellow grass, grey clay. And excrement, a smell that sometimes reached the house when the breeze blew from the east. In yards, behind hedges of organ cactus, the dust was kept alive by animals – chickens, pigs and, naked in their midst, the smaller children, whose excrement was prized by the livestock and the pariah dogs that huddled in patches of shade with their eyes burning. Everything was lean.

He and Isidro played in the half-shade of the pepper trees, gathering red pellets, playing marbles. Carolina, Isidro's pretty sister, watched them and never spoke a word.

At La Encantada, a dowdy prosperity survived. Don Raoul paced his room and the wealth, such as it was, found its way to his hands.

The people took their living from the soil. Don Raoul took his living from them. Deeds – properly certified – proved he owned the land. He owned the weather and the desert plain, the abandoned mountain and the people's huts. The peons had their rights, too: the right to be governed, to be protected.

And they had the little church. The priest kept to his patio as much as possible, emerging to say the services and do his office in the shadows.

Tio Alex said the little man had trained in Guanajuato at one of the great houses where vocation was tended among cypress trees and holy pictures. Each novice read books that promised challenges and, after ordination, went with hands outstretched, to collected the stigmata from a cloud. The cloud did not oblige. Or if it did, it did so slowly, subtly. The priest was just another exile.

In the church itself, the great banner of the Virgin, embroidered with gold thread, hung proudly, the sole rich possession of the congregation. They worshipped it, it was their common good. So were the lesser icons of the saints that they paraded on their holy days, spreading their concentrated magic in the smoky air after a day's work. The icons were stained with age and use, like the implements the men used in the fields. They were as close to hunger and the soil as the peons were. They became part of the land's furniture.

In his flock, the priest could smell the drought; if they grew old, their faces mirrored the chapped landscape, just as the children in the bad years wore the badness on their bodies. Bad years, he helped them plant children in bad soil, taking a few coins, a chicken, a basket of cactus fruit, to raise a stone or wooden cross. On the Day of the Dead he sold them votive candles for their vigils, and little sugar skulls.

It did not comfort the boy that he lay apart from them, hardly more alive than those they mourned with festive resignation. He knew so little about La Encantada and the people he would inherit. Profit and loss he could master – but as long as he rested in the debris of his room, he was a neutral presence at best. Better to abandon himself, the fragments of himself he had managed to recover. He was not really neutral – he had become a slow malignancy. It was time to move. The months in a wilderness of silence began to seem gestation.

The others were going completely – his mother, Isidro, his

uncle, and now Margarita. He must be there for something, wrapped in a sheet.

He made his way to the dark window, drew back the curtain with a finger and saw in the moonless sky all the stars Tio Alex had taught him. He opened the door and stepped into the air. The night was chilly. A breeze rustled the dry leaves. A faint glow showed where Santa Marta was, and far off, half-way to the horizon, a train brayed, and he thought he could see its glimmer.

29

It was summer and the cane was ripening, making the air dusty-sweet even at night. The house was restless, lights moving along passages and doors slamming. The boy looked out and was surprised to see his father, holding a lantern, unfastening the big locks on the Dresden gate. Far off he heard the jolting of wheels and a dark carriage loomed to a halt below him. Don Raoul gave a hand to a hunched little man and to a very large woman who carried with her a shapeless parcel. The little man gave the driver instructions, then they hurried in with Don Raoul. The front door slammed. The driver sat back, pulled his hat over his eyes, and fell asleep.

The boy went to his door and listened. They did not climb the stairs. There were other noises, all of them strange. Somewhere in the east wing, cries of a woman, muffled. He stepped into the hall and peered down the dim well. Marie moved through the hall with a basin. When she opened the door to the east wing, he heard another scream: '*Me muero!*' The door closed.

Then it was very quiet. The boy retreated to his room and heard his father climb to the lantern room. After an hour, Marie followed and brought him down again. It was almost dawn. He went to the gate and unbolted it. The little man and the large woman stepped into the early light, no longer in a hurry. The coachman woke and stretched, the horses snorted and he turned the carriage round. Don Raoul and the hunched man whose white hair stuck up in all directions stood talking, then Don Raoul handed him a small packet. The boy could hear the voices, not the words. With difficulty the large woman was hoisted into the carriage, and the old man followed. The vehicle began to roll towards Santa Marta.

Don Raoul closed the gate, then stood for a time looking after the cloud of dust, into the sun, dazed by the orange ball that climbed above the far hills of San Mateo.

When Marie brought the breakfast tray, the boy was sleeping. 'It is a son,' she whispered. He heard her strange voice and the blood rushed to his face. A son! By Margarita.

The birth changed him. His lethargy was over, replaced by an undefined energy. He was at risk, the past released him. That day he began to invent the time to come.

His father would die. Let him die briskly, painlessly, please God, with Paula's face rising before him as his eyes cloud. Let him forget the years of her absence and die gratefully. Well, he is dead, and the estates pass to his son. Which son?

The boy could hardly entertain the thought of it – a brother.

Here is the dark suit he wore for Tio Alex. The new vault is opened and another box set there to await resurrection. Tio Alex is glad of company. Brother by brother, they lie, *real* brothers made by the same parents in a large old place among vineyards and below which a sea broke on rocks.

A month of mourning and the boy moves upstairs, into the lantern room, leaving his place below vacant, the curtain closed as though a corpse was again laid out on the bed. When he takes his father's place, it is different, everything is different. Margarita and her bastard go. 'Goodbye, Margarita. Because you once loved me, here is money.' The dog is put down, a single shot at the base of the neck.

To begin with, he could go no further with his plans. Don Raoul was too vigorous for his inventions. He would not die so easily – the heavy tread of his pacing proved he was there, and had not sat down. The boy had forgotten the sound of his own voice – it was he who, with months of illness, had died. When he imagined his father's death, doubt asked, would the courtyard fill with his peons when the chapel bell tolled? When he came out on the steps, a heart of crape against his chest, would they acknowledge him as *patron?* Suppose they did, and he kissed the cheek of his dead father and addressed them, what then?

'The place is mine.' To do with as he pleased? No, pleasure

did not enter into it. He could do with the place what had been done before. His role was written for him in the big ledger books, in the large debts and the unpredictable seasons.

In one respect, he would be original. He would be the final master of La Encantada. After his solitude, he could not imagine the company even of a dog, much less a human touch. He would die without issue, ending in himself the sad history of his family and of the estates.

He remembered his new half-brother.

Don Raoul had not prepared him for the task of buying and selling, of living apart from common lives and turning aridity to some account. Unless a change came, his father might survive half a century more. A change, violent and clean. But the boy was still weak. He had no counsellor. Dreams came to him vividly, but they frightened him.

One in particular. He seemed to wake in the cane fields, near the village. Looking back towards the hacienda, he saw a red glow, like a large sunset ember. Before him he heard the villagers. They were not sleeping. In the centre of their little plaza was his table, the large table where Tio Alex had educated him. On the uneven ground the four legs did not touch the earth at the same time, and those who sat about it on his chairs tilted it towards them when they rose to speak. His lamp burned on the table and sharpened the features of each man. The light found reflection in their eyes, as though each had two burning wicks fuelled from the brain. They were arguing, but he could not understand them.

All that had been in his room was scattered through the village. In sleep, he understood the logic of possession by which they came there. The tall Obermuller portraits were hanging in the jacaranda tree, which had grown huge, making a canopy as wide as the great amate tree of San Mateo. In the breeze, the portraits swayed: it was like a tree of execution, or a Jesse tree. Time passed, but the things remained there, and where the great house was, an ember, glowing.

Inside the village chapel, a body was stretched across three chairs. The sanctuary light did not illuminate it, though the light glowed on the icons and made the whites of their upturned eyes appear. He thought the body was his father's. As he drew near to touch the cheek, the hand of the corpse moved up to brush the flies away. How fat it seemed. He saw not his father's face, but his own.

He woke but did not cry out. He found the room intact and the sun risen.

30

The dream stayed with him. It troubled him that he had not understood what the men were saying. They were like the men at the inn on the road to San Mateo.

His room was too narrow, too low. He wanted the air, the cane fields and the *campo*. He decided to recover, to make his legs work properly again and, step by step, to repossess the estates.

As far as his father knew, he still lay paralysed with illness. He preferred his father to remain deceived. He resolved to become a night creature. His peons would not see him yet, but he would know them well by the time he was free to go among them by day. He would creep from the house and take this road, that road, and learn again the disposition of the fields, how the cane was ripening and the maize. Each night, east and west, a shadow.

Since he was weak, to begin with he would walk only a little way – to the fountain, to the gate, and rest there, then return to his room. Gradually he would take in a mile, then two, enter the village again, though he had no friends there. The villagers would be asleep in their smoky hovels.

He dressed slowly. His feet seemed to have swollen. His body was loose and soft so that the clothes punished him. In the mirror, he saw a shapeless figure, hair grown to his shoulders, on his lip and cheeks a dense down. He took scissors and hacked off the hair, throwing handfuls into the grate. He found his uncle's old razor and scraped his beard. The mirror insisted: he was an unfamiliar creature.

The door was stiff on its hinges. Marie opened it just a crack to enter and depart, she was like a cat, slight and silent. Sometimes she left it ajar and the cool, musty smell of the passageway spilled in.

The village bell had told him it was Sunday. Before midnight he went to the door and listened, then into the hall. He tried the top stair, then the next, remembering the turning to the right where the mustiness gave way to freshness, for the old door had warped and the outer air flowed under it. Where his hand was braced against the wall, the flaking plaster caught under his nails. It was absolutely dark. He shivered. It was perhaps far enough for the first night? He went on.

The front door was not locked – there were no thieves at La Encantada, though there was hunger again. Habits of respect had survived the death of the just man. He had been too quiet. It was painful to start moving again, but there was pleasure in the pain. It was a kind of violation to move seriously for the first time outside the range of his father's will.

The front door was heavy. Like rolling back a boulder. And old, the wood black with age by daylight, at night cold and smooth as slate. He leaned against it with all his weight and it gave, inch by inch. And there, although it was midnight, the sky was brilliant after the darkness of the hall. Despite the hanging dust he was touched with health.

Don Raoul's light spilled from his room, a pale column on the cobbles. The boy skirted the light, though he knew that if his father were to look he could see little but reflections from the windows. The boy was part of darkness. He felt he should be nimble, with fear and expectation, but he moved clumsily. His fairness worried him; it was like a stain, an inadvertent torch. He should wear a dark hat to conceal it.

He skirted the courtyard, keeping to the wall, then along the blind arcade behind the orange trees. Trailing webs broke on his face. He heard rats scuttling, and a large fruit fell against his shoe. Breathing was hard in air pungent with decay.

Then the walled-up arches gave way to the open arch of the Dresden gate. Half a moon shone through it. The bars of the gate were cold: solid, eternal things. He saw the road stretch away to Santa Marta, and the starlit horizon more remote than in the day. 'It is ours almost as far as you can see,' Tio Alex had said when they stood there, surveying the dry hectares. To own so much desolation. It had amused him.

Standing alone, he reflected that it was his – rocks, dust, road, the gate and shadows cast by sunlight and moonlight; courtyard and house were his. When he moved to the lantern room, he would not light a lamp at night but keep it dark so he might see beyond his own face.

He was surprised to have gone so far on his first excursion. He was feverish, but his legs obeyed. Climbing the stairs again required unnatural effort. He fell on to his bed and slept all night there, still wearing his shoes.

He did the circuit each night until his legs were strong. One day he would be strong enough to go out beyond the side gate and around the north side, past the wing where Don Raoul and Margarita had their nest, on to the cane fields. One night he would go as far as El Abanico – not to the top, that was not possible, but to the ledge before the sheer cliff – and look across his property. Then he would know himself – like looking in a long mirror for the first time and seeing his body with new excitement.

Evening by evening he grew stronger. He slept during the day and they believed he was still ill. Marie did not report that his face grew thinner. She found his outdoor clothes thrown over a chair each morning, and his shoes covered with dust. She washed the clothes and polished the scuffed shoes.

He grew agile. Out of the mass of flesh emerged the spare body his illness had interred. This is how he would stand on the steps at his father's funeral, a young master like an Obermuller. He let his whiskers thicken on his cheeks and tried to trim his hair in the style of the portraits.

He no longer wandered vaguely among books. He read for information, and when he sat down, it was because he was tired. He left the curtains open all the time in order to watch. He learned the movements of the peons in the fields, and how the light altered from hour to hour. The rains began and maize grew, a green shadow covering the soil. Some nights there were storms. He watched them break over the house, and after midnight walked in them, regardless, and made his circuit of the courtyard.

The catch that held the side gate was easy, almost soundless, no noisier than when he bent his knee. At last he went beyond the cage of the Dresden gate. Outside the blind arcade, the stone facing was bare in moonlight. The moon made the house ruinous, heightening the weather's stains. He walked along the north side, passed the lighted window where Margarita sang to her baby in a voice that shook the boy – familiar songs and tones she had used years before. If the baby slept, she sang against loneliness. Don Raoul was in his room, spilling his beacon of lamplight.

The boy passed the chapel. He had not seen it by night. Beyond chapel and outbuildings – the cane fields. But no further, not yet, he was still learning. He strayed around the chapel. Someone had locked the door – locked and double-locked it. Perhaps the undertaker, after Tio Alex and Tia Thérèse were settled. The sanctuary light had at last burned out. The smell of bats was strong even at the bolted threshold. With his fingers he could reach the ledge of one window. He drew himself up with difficulty until he sat panting on the ledge. He looked inside. There was only darkness.

31

Now he was agile, moving from shadow to shadow, then pausing, advancing by sprints to the very edge of the tall cane fields. Wearing a black hat he had found among Tio Alex's things, and a black cloak which made him part of the night. He prepared to enter the sugar fields.

For weeks, he had thought about the expedition. To pass beyond the ground where gardens failed, the enclosure where the horses coughed and snorted, beyond walls and fences, trenches half-full of dust, into the whispering darkness of cane among which, in the day, men moved invisibly, their voices rising, singing, calling, like insects in deep grass, or birds.

The moon was out. He made his way by slivers of light that ribbed the ground. He started his inventory, lost behind a shivering wall of silver.

Late in the season, the canes were tall and full, many the thickness of a sturdy wrist. Breeze rubbed them against one another with a cracking as of knuckles. He heard rats, sudden alarm cries of birds.

Looking back, he could not make out where he had come from. As if at sea, the land moved off: here was an unfenced element, the spangling moonlight. He came home with wounds, incisions that the blades of cane left on hands, wrists and face.

He lay in bed next day. He was entirely a night creature now, his forays were like dreams. Each night he added to his inventory, learned the way to little clearings, forks and branches off the main paths (the fields were veined with trails along which the peons walked and off which at *zafra* time they began levelling the cane and bearing it in huge bundles on their backs). He cut sticks of cane and chewed them, swallowing the juice and spitting out the fibrous pulp.

Why were they not harvesting the cane? It was time for the *zafra* and past time. The canes burst with sap; a smell of fermentation filled the air.

Each night he came nearer to the village. The barking of dogs located it, the homely smell of wood-fires, the stench of excrement. One night he came across a little stream that ran towards the houses, opening a canal of starlight through the fields. A path ran along its bank. He was surprised at how pure it was – he could see the stones in the bottom – while, lower down, the women used it for their washing and it gathered the effluent of the place.

It made a pool that kept its warmth. He waded in and washed. After that, each night he stopped there, lay on his back in the water and watched the sky, then sat on a stone and let the night air dry him.

One night he heard noises, leapt naked from the water and crouched among the cane. Were there voices? Perhaps lovers – or bandits. He held his breath. The sound came closer – a careless crashing sound. There must be more than one – a troop of them perhaps. They had come for him.

He peered out of his brake. A donkey lurched into the clearing, ambled to the water's edge, stretched its neck out and drank. It was alone. When it had quenched its thirst, it raised its head. It brayed and brayed at the moon, at the stars, at its reflection.

The boy leapt from the cane, waving his arms, shouting '*Shoo!*' The donkey looked at him and kept on braying, as though he were not there. After a while, regardless of the boy, it put its head down and began foraging in the weed and grass along the bank. The boy found his clothes and dressed. He ran all the way back to La Encantada.

32

Waiting for night, he imagined the cane fields quite precisely, yet each time he actually entered them, he was surprised. He kept going back. By accumulating impressions, he might understand and eventually possess the world that was his due. He was glad of the bitter dust of the fields, unlike the dust that settled in his room. The night air was various temperatures – the slight pool of shade beside a wall, slivered warmth in the midnight fields, a sultriness in open places. At the heart of the cane fields, occasional storms wet him to the skin and filled his eyes with webs of lightning. And the gentler heat-lightning shuddered daylight along the horizon and seemed to threaten time, making the stars pale and the moon pewter, an erratic pulse through the air.

The village comprised two dozen dwellings clustered around a square with the squat church at one end. Some of the buildings had stone and adobe porches. In the square grew a jacaranda tree and some tulipans, the foliage stripped by ants. Pods of the jacaranda hung like castanets, releasing winged seeds that never rooted. A log served as a bench beneath the trees.

The boy stood at the edge of the village. There was no barking of dogs, as though he did not stand there in his body at all. Nothing stirred. It was after midnight and the moon cast long shadows. Wood-smoke clung to the roofs like wool. A child coughed. Still no dogs barked – it was as though the place was abandoned. He breathed the smell of habitation.

Half an hour passed and he saw little, and yet he had come to see just this, the sleeping village where for the Obermuller centuries, and perhaps for ever, those who belonged to the land of the big house had been born and lived – and from the little church had been sent on to the graveyard half a mile away.

His dream had been faithful to the little church – he had not set foot in it since his rides with Tio Alex. Small, doorless, ill-furnished except for the banner of the Virgin, it was half the size of the disused chapel at La Encantada. He entered it and knelt down at the back, raising his eyes to the dull sanctuary lamp. It gave no light but a point of warmth.

Yet light did fall on the wooden crucifix, a construction of sticks varnished and darkened with age and worship. He tried to pray, a jumble of words.

Dear sticks that stand for Christ's sacrifice, he began, apologizing for his neglect. He had not prayed at San Mateo, but here it was different, because his people prayed here. He asked to know Christ as the peons did. He prayed that his blood might run thicker and his skin turn dark. The great house would be Christ's if he might settle among the fleecy houses, poor among the poor, and help work the fields. Or give the peons something they did not have. Was he not born here? Was he not abandoned? He was an orphan and the land should claim him. How did the poor address Christ? He wanted to speak in their dialect, not as Brother Javier had tried to teach him. The peons prayed by rote and then by heart. They called the Virgin 'little Mother'. They had no language for irony or doubt.

The crossed sticks were bound together with a gold cord. No icon-figure hung there. The prayer he said was not quite what he meant. He wanted something more difficult than miracle. Prayer might change wine to blood, but never blood to blood.

How could he become wholly of the land? Kneeling there in his black hat and coat, he felt as pain the blondness of his hair, the blueness of his eyes.

The sleeping peons were like him in one respect: they belonged to his father. Yet when his father died, they would belong to him. He would occupy the lantern room, and they would bend their lives to the fields.

Don Raoul neglected them, and he neglected his son. If power was used differently, with love, the huts might yet become decent houses. If the *patron* would attend to the boy . . . The prayers should be directed to Don Raoul.

In the empty church, he clutched his hands together and

addressed the cross once more. No god would work miracles in this place: here, they would be squandered. Miracles happened where there were articulate witnesses, not among the poor unless the rich were near by. Instead of miracles, he would ask for the possible.

Make him hear. I shall *speak to him and change him. Not a big change: help me to set him back only a year.*

Leaving the church, the boy did not turn left into the cane fields but right, through the centre of the village, walking as a citizen. He headed up the gentle slope towards the foothills of El Abanico. In the dark he climbed the steep way, past the hill pasture where the skinny horses of the peons grazed. Following stone walls until they ceased, he went on the only way – a narrow path through untilled country, stars sometimes blocked out by cliffs and outcrops. It was a way that earthquakes readjusted, dropping a mountain, raising up a valley. Large stones compelled the path to zig-zag upward. Ahead, El Abanico was sheer, faceted like gypsum.

After two hours, wet with sweat, his heart thundering, he emerged on the ledge. Above him the mountain spread its fan a thousand feet, too sheer to scale. He looked back the dizzy way he had come. Moonlight turned the smooth stones of the path into a streambed, and the light flowed to the dark village and the silver fields. Deep in them the moon showed where the canals widened. Beyond, his dark house was reduced by distance to a kind of bruise. The *campo* was pale behind it, divided by bright undulations of the railway.

All this is mine, he said, *the maize and the* campo, *the cane and the parcelling walls.*

He spoke across space to his father's windows.

The path back should have been shorter but he lost his way and was overcome with fatigue. At last he found the village, and because morning was near, the dogs stirred and scented him. They broke the silence with their clamour and fear gave the boy energy to run. He had gone so far he thought it was a dream. But his shoes were scuffed from the ascent, his trousers and shirt damp and dusty. The knees of his trousers showed he had been kneeling.

How cold his room seemed after the night air. He closed the door just as the sun broke the line of the horizon.

33

He would talk to his father as soon as he could. He crossed himself and said his prayer again. There was no point in waiting. Don Raoul would be surprised: the boy was no longer a child. He was a young man. His father would embrace him as he had done when he returned from San Mateo, kiss him on both cheeks, pour out wine. The boy would not need to kill him.

Chiming filled his sunlit room like bird-song. It was noon. He dressed carefully, having trimmed his beard and splashed cold water on his face. His hair was blond like hay, his beard red-brown. Night walking had put colour in his face.

He climbed the stairs to the lantern room – only a year late for his appointment. Margarita was a poor mistress of the house. Dust lay thick on the stairs. The house had never been exactly clean, but such neglect – his father must have grown blind.

At the door he paused. It had always rather frightened him, even when as a child he went to summon his father down to dinner, or was admitted to lounge on the high sill and watch the birds' nests in the eaves.

Then he knocked. The dog growled and barked – not once but several times. There was no human reply. Again he knocked, and still no answer. He tried the handle but the lock was fixed. He hammered with his fist. In reply, above the barking, came a shout at the animal to be quiet, and then in the wake of its commotion a sound like an old man: 'Margarita?'

'No.'

The boy's unfamiliar voice passed through the door. Don Raoul approached him on the other side, the lock turned, he opened the door a crack. Then he opened it fully and stood with the light behind him. Light made him dark to his son, but the boy shone before him like an angel. Don Raoul chewed on a cigar.

'Who sent you? How did you get in?' He started to remember, a face and features rising from the past. When he knew, a shadow of pain crossed his face. He did not embrace the boy. He stood very still: here was a ghost from cancelled history, or Lazarus. They looked at one another.

Smoke wafted out like vapour from a cave. Don Raoul's beard was untrimmed, grizzled, his eyes bloodshot. His breath was stale with drink. Under his jacket he wore no shirt, only a frayed waistcoat and a knotted cravat pulled to one side. The dog at his heels bared her teeth.

The young man affronted him with his youth. Don Raoul's eyes narrowed.

'It is too late for this.'

'I have been ill. But I am better now.' The boy smiled.

'What do you want?' His voice was remote.

'Can we talk?'

'Of what?'

'May I come in?'

'The room is a mess,' he said, glancing over his shoulder. 'Say what you have to say out here.' He stepped on to the landing and closed the door. The dog howled on the other side. They stood in an echoing darkness where the boy could not see the full change in him.

'What have we to speak of?' The voice was dead – what had Margarita done to him? The boy thought of his prayer before the cross: it was not possible, there was nothing to be said to this man.

'What have we to speak of? I don't know. There must be something to say. How long have I lain ill? You are so changed! What makes you pace interminably back and forth?'

'How do you know I pace back and forth?'

'I can hear you, all day and half the night across my ceiling.'

'I shall try not to disturb you in future.'

'Disturb me, please,' the boy said, almost in tears. 'Tell me what is wrong! What is to happen? What are we to do?'

'*We* are to do nothing.'

129

'It is time I helped you.'

Don Raoul became impatient. 'The time for that is past. I have other plans.'

The boy descended the stairs slowly, expecting at each moment that his father would call him back. He did not call. He disappeared into his room and slammed the door so hard that a shower of dust and plaster fell in the corridor below. Soon his pacing resumed. The boy sat before the hearth trembling, not with rage but recognition. The place was not to be his – the fields, the village, the house, the hills and mountains, not his. He was the dead son; Margarita had borne the heir.

If Paula should return, even with age's cankers on her, her husband would know her; but she would not know him, or if she did she would see that her enchantment had worn off and he had surrendered to a large failure. The boy was filled with pity. He would try a second time. After all, his father had been unprepared. He had seen a sort of ghost.

He climbed the stairs once more. This time Don Raoul would not be surprised. He would have had a time to reflect. The boy knocked and the dog began her furious barking.

'Margarita?'

'No, it is me.'

There was a silence that seemed long, then footsteps, the dog growling. He opened the door three or four inches.

'If you do not keep to your room, I will take care of you. I have problems.' He pointed the barrel of a pistol through the door, drawing back the hammer with his thumb. 'Go away. If you need anything, ask Marie.'

'What have I done?'

Don Raoul did not answer – again the door slammed. The boy heard a light tread at his back. Margarita came out of the stairwell.

'What is the matter with him?' asked the boy.

He stood back to let her pass. She wore a red gown and tossed her head as though she had not seen him before, and it was an impertinence for him to address her. How old she looked! A woman with deep rings around her eyes, and heavy-set.

'Margarita!'

She avoided his eye, though she cast a sidelong glance of fear and triumph at him. She tapped lightly on the door and was admitted.

Now it was over. His father had drawn new borders in his world. They excluded the boy.

He would have to take what would not now be given. He had learned in the last weeks a hunger for possession, and now he was free to hate Don Raoul. He felt grateful to his father: he had freed him by rejecting him.

Don Raoul's pacing no longer troubled the boy. They located his foe. Hatred was a foretaste of action. It was not only that Don Raoul had held a gun: his face had changed, it offered no prospect of acceptance. The father was dead. The woman, too, should suffer. If he had skill, he would seduce that woman who walked about the house in clothes his mother brought from France. He had no skill. His nurse was dead.

From his window, he watched the backs of the peons in the fields, the wink of their machetes in the sun, or the long sad road to Santa Marta; or he sat listlessly before the hearth or at the spinet where he touched the untuned keys. A mute rage filled him. He wanted revenge, like in the old Spanish plays – revenge on the usurper who used his father's body, ran its hand through his father's hair, disowned his father's son. 'I am awake,' he said aloud, and took down from the wall the rusted pistols.

34

They were duelling pieces and had belonged to the Obermullers, as had the sabres and the blunderbusses elsewhere,
among the more sedate hangings. The boy found rags, an old
tin of oil, balls and powder in the cupboard where his uncle
used to keep hunting gear in careful order. The pistols were
ceremonial, handles inlaid with mother of pearl, hammers
formed like sword-hilts.

Guns for men wealthy enough to have honour! The boy
turned them in his hands, admiring the patterns and the grip.
They lay snug in each palm. But the spring on one of them was
broken. He took the other. Though scaled with rust, he thought
he could make it work. He took it to pieces and began,
remembering his uncle's routine, and how he had helped
prepare for the casual shoots they went on, loading the car-
tridges and running the long brush down the barrels of their
rifles, while Tio Alex told stories about stalking and riding to
hounds. They brought home wiry birds that were served up and
chewed, not really eaten; and iguanas that Marie prepared in
fillets so they tasted like sweet pork. Once they had shot a
wildcat and would have kept the pelt, but it was so verminous
they had to burn it in the end. Its smell clung about the pantries
for weeks.

He tore up an old shirt for extra rags, took oil and polished
the instrument piece by piece. He forced the barrel clean – it
was clogged with web and dust. He oiled the hammer and it
clicked into place. On the writing table he spread the materials
for making the ammunition, piling finished rounds on the
writing paper Tio Alex had left tidily beside his pens. The boy

did not remove his uncle's things, though the ink well was dry. Most of what he left kept its place, refusing to acknowledge his departure.

By evening the boy held a serviceable weapon in his hand and had enough ammunition in his jacket pocket for the task he planned. Before he used the gun, he must test it in the open.

Marie brought his dinner and overlooked the confusion of his room. He ate hungrily, surveying the debris of preparation: oil-stained tatters in the grate, smudges on the carpet, and on the wall the pale oblong where the gun had hung unmolested for years, above the clock that chimed eleven times before he stepped into the dark corridor.

What if Don Raoul should suddenly mellow and descend to seek him, his heart relaxed with wine, and find the boy's room empty? The possibility crossed his mind as he passed the chapel on his way to the fields – the face of Don Raoul as he had seen it that day, his voice. Was there a chance of such a visit? He remembered his prayer to the village cross. It might be answered. He returned to his room.

Midnight passed. One o'clock. Don Raoul paced back and forth. At two his foot sounded on the stairs. Descending, he did not hesitate even for an instant at the boy's door. He went down, towards the east wing, and his steps faded.

The boy made his way to the heart of the cane fields, to the stream. Tonight the water did not tempt him: it offered an open stretch, space in which a bullet could fly. He loaded the gun and held it before him in both hands, pointing into the dark further shore. The gun kicked upward with a flash of light. Dogs in the village erupted into life. The weapon was in order.

The boy's arms tingled. He walked further, to the edge of the cane fields. Squatting in the dark he gazed towards the village. The dogs, barking still, stayed close to the houses. Something was happening in the crude plaza – a large fire burned under the jacaranda and the tulipan trees, lighting the scarred trunks and the men busy among them, moving to and fro, and voices raised not in conversation but in loud, quick exchanges. There was no hearth smoke about the roofs, only the acrid smell of the big fire.

It was late – they should have been asleep. Perhaps it was a festival – All Souls'? He did not know what day it was, what month.

Their horses were saddled; some carried large burdens on their backs. Women squatted by the walls, dozing and watching, a few babies in shawls and children sleeping at their feet.

The boy clutched his pistol at his chest and stayed there, trying to overhear them. He was too far away to distinguish words. He was tempted to go forward and speak with them, but a shyness – it was not like fear – restrained him. He had no sense of danger, but alarm: Did Don Raoul know of this or did they too now move beyond the borders of his will?

Returning through the cane field the boy reloaded his gun and stood still in the narrow path. He steadied the weapon and fired again into the cane. A flight of birds burst upward at the discharge, and once more the village dogs barked and howled. The birds wheeled like ash into the faintly lighted upper air. An orange glow from the village hung in the sky behind him, and before him rose the dark chapel, the house not quite asleep after all. His father's room was illuminated.

Don Raoul had gone to bed and risen again almost immediately. He was looking towards the village. He could see little but the glow. He heard the gun discharged; his dog barked too and would not be silenced. He gazed out with the window thrown wide open, both hands on the sill, a sentinel. The boy waited in the shadows until he went away.

Entering at the footgate, he turned left instead of right – a fortunate precaution. Out of the front door came Don Raoul, on his wrist a ring of keys. He closed the side gate through which the boy had come. With difficulty he turned the key in the rusted lock. He took a larger key and closed the second lock on the Dresden Gate itself. Then he stood back and surveyed the blind arcade, as a captain might look over a fortification. He breathed heavily as he moved, muttering, confiding only in himself. Then he went in. Once more his face appeared at the upper window, gazing towards the village and the reddish glow. His skin was coloured by that light that spread now from the village to the fields of over-ripe cane. There was no breeze; the brightness crept slowly along the east.

There was no village now. The villagers were driving their laden horses up the pass to the south of El Abanico. The women followed with their sleeping burdens. The priest, hands bound behind him, stumbled after. Unfurled at the head was the gold-embroidered banner of the Virgin.

Don Raoul had not locked the house door. The boy went in. From where he had been hiding, he could not see the spreading flames.

35

He woke at ten. The sun was in his room like a fine haze. Dust lay on everything, confining it irrecoverably to the past. He had left the window open all night long. Sunlight was colourless and blinding, smelling of smoke. Tiny curls of ash blackened his pillow.

Tonight he would kill Don Raoul. The weapon was proven. If he had the courage, he would kill Margarita, too, taking two bullets, recharging while she waited. He thought of her, dead beside her lover in candlelight, the baby waking, its little voice, the butt of the pistol once, hard, on the skull. Mother of pearl.

So that Marie would not notice what he had done – now he was ready to act, he was afraid of detection – he hung the gun in its old place against the pale print it had left on the wall. He gathered the debris and pushed it in a drawer. Time passed slowly. The air was strange with ashes. But the fire had burned out on the eastern ridge. He saw a long swathe of black, like a shadow, and smelt burned sugar.

Marie was fretful when she came. She spoke one of her rare phrases under her breath. 'So much dust, so much death.' She looked tired and very old.

'Are you unwell, Marie?'

She gathered dust up in a cloth and shook it from the window, then drew the curtains.

When she left, he pulled the curtains back, re-opened the window and sat at the table, looking out. Men were active in the fields. Were they hoeing? They worked in groups, which was unusual – normally they moved singly along the furrows. They went slowly, as if talking while they poked at the ground with their implements. Where was Don Pepe? The boy did not recognize all the faces that sweated in the field.

Don Raoul, like the boy, looked from his window, standing slightly to one side so as not to be seen. He was waiting – for Don Pepe? for the train? The gate remained locked. There were still horses in the stables, flight was not impossible. Yet this did not settle the unease he felt. They were opening his grave in the fields.

Just after noon, a military train screamed to a halt at the station. A dusty detachment of Federals tumbled out, their lean horses led neighing out of goods wagons and saddled. A column formed and moved briskly towards the house. The train coughed and started up again, making its way to Santa Marta with reinforcements and provisions for the town.

Don Raoul hurried down, no longer the tired wanderer between indecisions. He threw open the door, ran to the gate, fumbled with the keys. Both leaves of the great gate folded back as he tugged them – he, the *patron*, without a servant to open his gate!

Fifty men on horseback. The courtyard clattered under a hail of hoofs. The boy opened his window to hear the voices raised above the uproar of arrival. The captain did not dismount but talked down to the dishevelled *hacendado*. He was a well-spoken officer and rode erect, a gentleman, unlike his conscripts who slouched comfortably in their saddles like peons.

There was trouble north and south, he said. It might reach here, it might already be here. The boy looked at the men in the fields who had stopped working and watched from under the shadows of their hats.

How bad was the trouble? Don Raoul reported the previous night's fire to the east.

He was to bring in his trusted servants and peons, lock the hacienda and arm himself.

Trusted peons – the faces in the fields, in the stables, in the kitchen – trusted? He nodded.

The Lebrun estates were ashes, their overseer had vanished and was feared dead. At least he had got the harvest in. At La Encantada the harvest had not begun.

Don Raoul begged a dozen men from the captain – only a dozen, only half a dozen. He would keep and feed them. There was real trouble here. Ever since El Manantial had gone up in smoke and the people had gone into the hills, taking horses, livestock . . . half a dozen men.

It was not possible.

Was La Encantada the last *hacienda* untouched by the troubles?

There were some others. They were riding out to warn them.

Three armed men would do.

Impossible. But if he liked, the captain said, stroking his pale moustache, Don Raoul and his people could come away with the detachment on its return. It would mean surrendering house and land to the spreading flames.

'When do you return?'

'Tomorrow, or the next day – when we have completed the circuit of El Abanico.'

'We will come away with you when you return.'

The captain made a little speech: until he returned, they were to be vigilant. Not even an army could guarantee property and safety at this time. It would require a winged horse to carry them beyond the borders of the sad Republic. There was revenge in this uprising, a blood hunger. The leaders were not gentlemen, their troops were brutal, hungry men. Nothing was spared, not even the Church. The ruins of San Mateo were eloquent.

'What time shall we expect you?'

'I cannot say exactly. Prepare yourself. We will take you with us. The train is expected two days from now, around sunset.'

'Which way do you go now?'

'Along the pass.'

'It is a dangerous way.'

Any way was dangerous. When the guns were out, how quickly the bad dream returned.

The captain turned his horse and galloped out, followed by his men. For a time they were lost in a cloud of dust, then they reappeared to the east, bound for the steep ascent where the boy had gone on his nocturnal survey. The line of men grew smaller. Now they seemed spiders moving on a thread that stretched upwards towards the ledge of El Abanico. They galloped, but the distance made them almost still. And then they vanished behind boulders.

Don Raoul closed the Dresden gate and locked it. The peons in the fields stood still and watched. Don Pepe was nowhere to be found. The peons stood as if asleep on their feet, the whip that drove them set aside for now. Then they began to disappear in little groups, for the afternoon drew on and the sun was setting. Darkness drew up its lid of starlight. The boy still had his plan. Overhead he heard his father's footsteps now purposeful. He was gathering what he would take in flight, objects he could not part with, packing his bags to leave exile at last.

36

Far off, the boy could hear Margarita's endless lullaby, or was it the breeze through the gateway, or further off a chorus of voices thinned by distance to a clear, wavering music? He rubbed the pistol with a scrap of flannel. The cavalrymen might not return next day, or ever. The riders were untrained, common men; a large event might free them from their oaths to the Republic. They might return with the privilege of their uniforms, taking booty casually. Yet Don Raoul believed the officer. All at once he seemed anxious to live. Perhaps he believed he could return to France when his failure was not on his own head. 'The revolution came, we could not stay; we were doing well, but they took everything.'

The boy waited. Would Don Raoul never descend to Margarita? He continued winnowing his possessions. Would he try to take her as well? The boy's plan was simple but he did not feel secure in it. The surrounding fields and mountains had altered overnight. He was frightened. If only his father would come through the door and speak, the boy's plan would vanish in an instant. 'Take no risks,' the captain had said, and Don Raoul had fastened every opening. There was a foe within, a warrior hidden in the belly of a horse. The fact that his father did not suspect him made his action the more difficult.

The clock chimed the half hour – half past two. Don Raoul's step slowed, he moved across to his door, muttered to the dog, which stayed on guard. A key turned in the lock and he descended. The boy held his breath. His father did not pause. The light of his lamp moved along the cracks around the door, and then the cracks grew dark. The boy rose and followed with no light down the stairs and kept always one turning in the corridor behind him. He had forgotten how large the house was; they moved out from the old part of the building along cold passageways into the east wing. Mirrors lined the walls; he kept glimpsing his retreating father who moved slowly, like a sleep-walker. It was late – too late to start again.

He stopped before a door. The boy realized that the corridor had been filled all the while with her voice, singing; she was a siren who sang not a lullaby but a charm to draw him from his tower to the ground. He tapped, her voice stopped and she opened to him. The door closed.

Moving forward, feeling his way along the mirrors, the boy drew the pistol from his belt. He pressed an ear to the door. He looked through the keyhole into the dark. They had passed into a further room. He tried the door and it opened into the unlighted ante-room. He stumbled on a low table and a clock overturned, chiming and shattering on the stone floor. From the room beyond, Margarita cried out, answered by the shrieking of the baby. '*Quien va?*'

The boy fled. Don Raoul burst into the ante-room with his lantern, calling out. The boy was barefoot and made no sound as he fled. Although he was as good as blind, he found the way, directed by fear. Back in his room, he shut the door quietly. The dog upstairs was barking. The boy was glad to find he had the pistol still. He knew they would come for him. He had again broken into his father's closed life.

He leapt into his uncle's bed and feigned sleep.

After some minutes, the door handle turned, a hemisphere of light advanced into the room, his father's face appeared in the glow, gazing here and there. He approached the bed.

The boy held the pistol ready, just under the covers by his heart. Providence was granting him a second chance. Don Raoul came to his bedside and stood looking down. The boy's eyes were open just enough to see his father studying him, turning to the shelves of books, brushing his hand across the bindings. He walked once around the room, glancing from the window, pausing to touch, to hear. He returned to the bed, watching the boy's face, reluctant to leave, tempted it seemed to wake him and speak. The face of Margarita emerged into the light. She was afraid since he had left her for so long. She saw

141

Don Raoul before he noticed her and she could read him. She looked at the boy with hatred.

'Come away,' she whispered. 'It is not this one.'

They left him. Later the dog fell silent. But the wailing of a child continued, distant but penetrating the corridors and passages. It made the boy cry too, holding the pistol tight against his chest.

37

Next day he slept and slept. The horsemen did not come back. At evening Marie brought dinner. He dressed and sat at his table. There was a total stillness in the view. No creature moved and the sun was low, extending shadows, making furrows deep as canyons, long, flowing with darkness. Gradually the flood covered the *campo*, only the sky staying slightly pale. There was no moon. The train would come back tomorrow.

Eternity was like this long habitual supper, alone, watching his hands, the steam in the cup die down, the candle eat itself. He looked into the recesses of the room. On the wall opposite, the candle flame just caught a painting of a place that was in sunlight. He sat still. What moved in the darkness? There were rasping sounds. Not crickets, but metallic rasping. Without hunger, he dipped the bread. Marie came for the tray, he slept again, heavily, without dreams.

Marie did not come with his breakfast. He woke at eight, rose and dressed with special care, as though for a serious day. Still Marie did not come. He grew annoyed. Ten o'clock. He went to the door and called for her. In the cool hall, not even an echo answered.

The place had the air of being sealed, each door and window with the lid drawn down. Marie was gone.

Noon, and then afternoon, the fields deserted, no shrill voice of Don Pepe, no hats bobbing by the walls or flash of machete blades, no laden donkeys on the rutted road to Santa Marta. Up towards El Abanico, the only movement was of black birds circling and diving, a dance of ashes.

He threw the window open. A stifling air came from the

campo. He had not heard the peons' night words but he had understood them – such weather, and their hovels, the sparse food yielded by the fields, the cuts and scars of cane, the deaths, the exigent Lord God – how they were tired not only in themselves but in their history, with the gathered tiredness of their ancestors in their bones, turning to rage. They withdrew. He wished he had gone with them. How Don Pepe and the *patron* must have driven them that they should abandon even their dead! And Marie was gone. The house was empty, the fields were empty. He was filled with sadness, then with fear again.

His father was waiting for the captain in the lantern room. No longer pacing, no longer hoping. He waited, looking towards the hills. 'Tomorrow afternoon' was yesterday. He too saw the dance of ash, the black birds above El Abanico. They moved west by degrees, towards the pass.

Who was coming? A column of blown dust ran down the road, then spun into a funnel and jumped the wall. Don Raoul rested his hands on the sill. He knew his land, its yield in maize and cane. During the rare good years he loved it gratefully, but when it failed he loathed the stones of the house, the men, the very soil. His eldest son had been born there, as the peons had been. He no longer cared either for the men or for his son.

While Don Raoul despised his peons, the boy understood them. He shared their tyrant. If he went to them in the hills and said, 'Show me how you work,' would they receive him? He had a pistol in his belt. If he could free them of their tyrant, would they welcome him? He could still kill Don Raoul, not out of revenge, not for his property. By killing he would renounce all material claims. He would kill for them. They were too weak, too poor to rise against their master. He was not one of them – he was more free, and they would take his sacrifice.

He thought of Don Raoul's tyranny – a tyranny of greed. His death might lead to a tyranny of virtue, purging the land of excess and imbalance. If there was hunger (and there would be hunger) it would be shared. Virtue would grow sinewy. No charity or pity would be required.

If in time the place prospered again, no one would rejoice above the rest. Life would be a confluence of wills, and the large house of La Encantada would become a mound of rubble like the mine that crowned El Abanico. The boy would call them back out of the hills, step into the courtyard with his pistol smoking, in his hand the keys to the Dresden gate.

38

They *were* returning. They came as if summoned by his thoughts. His heart swelled at the sight of them far off, emerging from the southern pass, above them the black birds circling like angels over a ritual procession.

Far off, they looked festive, more in number than he thought the village had held. Perhaps they were joined by men from El Manantial, by Isidro even, who must still remember him. They came on horseback. At the head, one bore the gold embroidered banner and it shone, the Virgin on a cactus ground. Others brought smaller banners, but she floated over them all. As at Troy, attentive gods hovered above their champions.

The boy applauded their return. Before he could see their faces he was smiling. He heard shouting, chanting. He was weak with expectation.

As they drew nearer he saw unknown faces with large hats pushed back, cheeks bristled with a few days' beard, eyes and skin dulled by dust. Three men dragged curious burdens behind their horses – three bodies tied with rope, bouncing on the stones, as if they were the riders' shadows, clad in Federal colours. They had been dragged so far that they were hardly bodies any longer – broken things the flies sucked hungrily. Which was the captain? Their features had been erased. Certainly the skinny horses ridden by the loud, large-hatted men were Federal horses, and the bright carbines were those the soldiers had carried. Where were their comrades – spilled somewhere along the skirt of El Abanico, or had they joined their enemies? The boy could not conceive of those dragged, blue-clad bundles as dead men. They had hardly a differentiated limb except the leg by which they were pulled. They were not like Hector. Because the boy could not put a face to them, he felt only disgust, as at some poor representation of a violent act, and not the thing itself.

The procession reached the Dresden gate. There were many more there than at Tio's funeral. Their leaders did not dismount. The man who bore the Virgin aloft swayed her to and fro, while those who had materialized on foot came forward and rattled the tall gate. The landscape was full of people, they sprouted there; from behind stone walls, out of furrows, women and children rose, old men stepped from the cover of cactuses. It was a field of people, the earth spat up its dead. Not all of them were from the neighbourhood. There were too many to count, there at the gate and filling the road far back, all shouting now separately and now, terrifyingly, in unison. Some prodded the dragged bodies, others turned their full attention on the living. They looked up to Don Raoul's window. By the way they looked, the boy knew his father stood gazing down on them, remote, higher than the brocade madonna. He held the space above as a god they were intent to bring down.

When they had been far off, the boy had rejoiced with them as with a just idea. Now that they stood armed below, with the fly-blown dead, the pistol in his hand seemed heavier, the chiming of his clock more tentative. They were too numerous, too single-minded. What word would penetrate their ears? They were embarked and could not be delayed. He told himself again they were justly angry. Yet their anger seemed to include him. They were not bad men, though staring and shouting at the gate they seemed so – not bad but evil, stifling one another in one air that wafted up to the boy, acrid. Between them and the house was the great courtyard, the quiet cobblestone flower and, in the centre, like a font, the fountain with its covering of weeds. They perceived the open space and wished to fill it with themselves. If in that space were treasures, heirlooms, books and pictures that traced a history that had used them as a potter uses clay, they with their human shapes would displace those artfacts. What had been stolen from their labour was theirs to do with as they wished.

They shook fists at the upper window. Then all at once, with a giant's voice, they made their cry. The boy shouted with them, out loud, as if he shared their purpose. He clutched his pistol knowing he could free them. They had not meekly moved off from Babylon – they had come back to take it for themselves. He loved them for it (except the strangers there). He smiled, standing in his window above the multitude of brothers.

They watched him as they watched his father. 'The little motherless *patron!*' one of them shouted. *'Hija de puta!'* He was within range of their slings. A window shattered, the ancient blue glass spilled about him and his brow was grazed. He looked down paralysed: his mouth made words but in the din they were inaudible. They had drawn blood. He stepped back, crunching the glass like gravel under his heels.

'The *patron!* Give us the *patron!*'

He did not hear his door open. His father stood beside him. He had trimmed his beard and dressed well. He looked almost as he had when the Lebruns had come to call – elegant, still rather young, a gentleman. He was drawing on his gloves. He wore his riding boots with silver spurs. Behind him, her tongue lolling, came the dog, trembling, unable now to bark.

'Give us the *patron!*' they shouted.

'There is no one to give them the *patron*,' said Don Raoul, 'except the *patron* himself. The others have all gone, just as your mother did.'

'All of them?'

'This morning Margarita was not there. The child went with her. Don Pepe vanished days ago. Marie left last night and took what valuables she could carry. The house is empty. But you are still here.' He spoke rapidly, as though there were an intimacy between them, as though he had been absent a few minutes only, not for years. There was no time to waste. He saw the cut above his son's eye, took the handkerchief from his breast pocket and wiped the blood from his face. 'Only a scratch,' he said.

Now the boy could have done it, pulled the trigger, taken the body down and handed it to those faces as a token, to buy their favour and his restitution.

'She has left you too?' the boy asked.

'With all she could lay her hands on. She was a strong woman, to flee with a baby and a pile of loot that high!' He laughed. 'She will find few friends in this neighbourhood. Perhaps with Pepe she has gone to the capital.'

'She took the baby.'

His father was not listening. He looked at the crowd pushing at the gate and wall.

'They will break in soon.'

'Where shall we go?'

'Down. I have to go to them. You had better stay where you are.'

He folded the handkerchief and put it back in his breast pocket. He embraced the boy and kissed him on both cheeks.

Followed by the dog, he left, closing the door behind him. The boy heard the spurs ring on the stairs as he passed down through the dark, cool passage. 'Where shall we go?' he asked the empty room. Three times he might have killed him, the third time there beside him in the room. The gun weighed him down. It could have given him wings, a single shot. Yet, as the footsteps receded, he did not hate Don Raoul. He was waking up. He was no longer an orphan. Better for them to do it than for the son. His father unbolted the front door.

'I had rather close my own lips on the barrel of this gun than kill him.'

39

When Don Raoul appeared on the steps, the crowd beyond the gate fell silent. He closed and locked the door with two large keys. He knew he would not enter his house again. He lighted a cigar there on the steps, flicked the match on to the cobbles and gazed at his adversaries from their level.

'They will shoot him.'

They did not shoot. Calmly, with the dog at his heels, Don Raoul moved across the courtyard to the gate. It was a wall of faces, fingers, toes – boys had scaled it and clung all the way to the top, at the very keystone of the arch.

'Who is the leader?' called Don Raoul in a loud voice, his accent sounding strange thus magnified.

There was some shuffling, then a red-faced horseman he had never seen before growled, 'We have no leaders, but I will speak for them, if they wish.'

'Speak for us!' they cried together.

'I do not know you. What do you want here?'

'What we have been calling for!' He turned his face to the crowd and scowled at them; they cried their slogan as one: 'Land! Land! Liberty! Liberty!'

Don Raoul raised a hand to silence the crowd. Such was the residual respect for custom that they fell silent.

'How can I give you land and liberty?'

'You cannot give them to us. We have come to take them.' Another roar of approbation.

'I will speak to some of you. We can arrange terms. You will allow me and my son to go.'

'Open the gate!' the sullen horseman said.

'Open the gate!' they echoed him. 'Open the gate and let the *pueblo* in!'

For a moment Don Raoul hesitated. If he turned and walked back to the house, they would shoot him in the back. He had no choice but to stay facing them.

'I will entertain a small delegation, but no more.'

'Three or four of us, then. We will confer,' the self-appointed spokesman said. 'We want no treachery.' His eyes surveyed the house as though he thought an ambush was prepared.

'I am unarmed.'

Then Don Raoul took the large keys from the ring and fitted them in the locks of the main gate. The crowd was silent, the boy could hear the keys turn in the fine old mechanisms, the click of part engaging part. The long metal tongues withdrew until, with a creak, the left leaf of the gate began to open. With a surge the crowd burst the right gate open. Four horsemen surrounded the *patron*. The courtyard filled with men and women, as at the wakes when an Obermuller died.

The horsemen dismounted. They tied the *patron*'s hands. Still he clenched the cigar between his teeth, his spurs sang as he was led across the cobbles – sang even above the commotion of the crowd. He was led to the blind arcade. Under an arch, the sunlight in his eyes, they hobbled him tight as they hobbled their horses. There they left him with his eyes uncovered. Still he was smoking his cigar. He stood as if nonchalantly resting beside one of the twisted orange trees. The dog sat down beside him.

He looked above his captors' heads at the boy's window. He called out, but the words did not reach his son's ears. The cigar fell smouldering at his feet. Then a fan of vacancy opened before him, he was left framed with his dog beneath the archway. Six men knelt with rifles at their shoulders (this at least they had learned from the Federals). He was staring at the boy's window. His body folded. Then the report of the guns reached the boy's ears, and the crowd was still. He could hear the dog whimper, then she turned to sniff Don Raoul's hand.

The boy was dizzy. He left his vantage and stepped into the hall, hurried up the stairs to the lantern room. It was now his, though it retained the smell of his father's cigars, of his anxiety. The papers were in disarray – a moment before, he was alive.

Here were his bags packed as if for travel. Well, he had gone without them.

The view! It was so vast from here, so clear! Yet all he saw to the south was flatness and, below him, the people of the flatness and his father's body. They were taking off his spurs. They were undressing him. He was abandoned as a seedhusk among ants.

Now there was smoke. They had lighted torches. The heat of the day was not sufficient, they needed fire. The house was strong against them; they had not yet broken down the heavy door. They set the yellowed window shutters alight, the shutters his father had hung to please a wife, 'to translate this Prussian into French'. They burned like tinder, each window on the front was framed in fire, but the walls were stone and did not catch.

The front door began to burn at last. A little longer still it would hold. At his father's window – at *his* window – he stood above the flames. Don Raoul lay below and, outside the gate, the three corpses of the Federals were abandoned now. Far off towards Santa Marta, with little gouts of smoke, the military train was making its way across the *campo*, as if it were just another Tuesday.

The boy belonged to them, to the *pueblo!* He tried to forget his father in the courtyard. When they burst into the house, surprising their own faces in the mirrors, he would cry out – in an accent slightly coloured by his upbringing – *Long live the Revolution!* He would descend with them into the burning courtyard of his house and offer them his hand. They would surely welcome him among them.

Or he would sit quite still at the window, staring north to El Abanico and the mine whose circling walls still looked to him like a castle, suspended above the rustling cane, and turning up his eyes take in that blue, that cooling distance.

He had a choice: he could go down, he could sit still.